## "TAKE OF[F YOUR SHIRT,"
## SA[ID MRS. MURRAY.

Slocum hesitated, but there was no way out of it. He put down the carpenter's tools and removed his shirt. Then he resumed his sawing.

Mrs. Murray began a charcoal sketch of him. "Very good trapezoids," she said, then added, "but your back is covered with scars."

"Horse threw me onto a roll of barbwire," Slocum lied.

"Please remember," Mrs. Murray said coldly, "that I've been an army wife for a long time. Those are bullet wounds. Either you've been shot at by a coward—or a posse. What do you say to that?"

*I'd say,* thought Slocum, *that you are a very dangerous woman....*

## OTHER BOOKS BY JAKE LOGAN

RIDE, SLOCUM, RIDE
HANGING JUSTICE
SLOCUM AND THE WIDOW KATE
ACROSS THE RIO GRANDE
THE COMANCHE'S WOMAN
SLOCUM'S GOLD
BLOODY TRAIL TO TEXAS
NORTH TO DAKOTA
WHITE HELL
RIDE FOR REVENGE
OUTLAW BLOOD
MONTANA SHOWDOWN
SEE TEXAS AND DIE
IRON MUSTANG
SHOTGUNS FROM HELL
SLOCUM'S BLOOD
SLOCUM'S FIRE
SLOCUM'S REVENGE
SLOCUM'S HELL
DEAD MAN'S HAND
FIGHTING VENGEANCE
SLOCUM'S SLAUGHTER
ROUGHRIDER
SLOCUM'S RAGE
HELLFIRE
SLOCUM'S CODE
SLOCUM'S FLAG
SLOCUM'S RAID
SLOCUM'S RUN
BLAZING GUNS
SLOCUM'S GAMBLE
SLOCUM'S DEBT

# JAKE LOGAN
## SLOCUM AND THE MAD MAJOR

**PLAYBOY PAPERBACKS**

SLOCUM AND THE MAD MAJOR

Copyright © 1982 by Jake Logan

Cover illustration copyright © 1982 by PEI Books, Inc.

All rights reserved. No part of this book may be reproduced, stored in a retrieval system or transmitted in any form by an electronic, mechanical, photocopying, recording means or otherwise without prior written permission of the publisher.

Published simultaneously in the United States and Canada by Playboy Paperbacks, New York, New York. Printed in the United States of America. Library of Congress Catalog Card Number: 81-85824. First edition.

Books are available at quantity discounts for promotional and industrial use. For further information, write to Premium Sales, Playboy Paperbacks, 1633 Broadway, New York, New York 10019.

ISBN: 0-867-21217-9

First printing July 1982.

# 1

Toward the end of April 1882, a hard-bitten, exhausted rider on a fine chestnut dismounted on a mountain trail considerably south of Benson in southeastern Arizona. He stared ruefully at the bullet hole centered neatly in the cantle of his saddle; then he smiled and shrugged. A little creek foamed beside the narrow trail. He took off his battered sombrero and lay prone. A five-foot length of old timber had drifted to one side of the creek. Slocum spread out his arms on the plank and bent his head to drink.

Two bowstrings twanged from the slope behind him. Before Slocum could react, two arrows pinned his palms flat against the wood. With all the strength of his wide shoulders, Slocum tried to snap the shafts, tried to raise up and then fall sidewards. But his outstretched arms did not provide any leverage. The arrowheads had gone too deeply into the wood. There was nothing to do but wait for death, which would be a long drawn-out business in this country of the Chiricahua Apaches.

He tensed his body against the expected additional strum of the bowstrings. Nothing happened. His horse was still drinking placidly from the creek. Slocum hoped that his death would be quick.

Sure enough his captors were Chiricahuas. There were six of them, sliding jubilantly down the slope in a cascade of dust and small pebbles. They stood around him, grinning. They were dark and squat like Comanches but not so broad of chest. Their hair hung down to their shoulders. Filthy white cotton handkerchiefs served as sweatbands. Two wore U.S. Cavalry blouses. Each blouse had a ragged hole in the back, edged with dried blood. One man was bare-chested; the other three wore cotton blouses that had obviously been looted from a wagon train. All wore dirty white breechclouts and supple Apache boots that they wore pulled up to their knees in the spiny chaparral. None of them had a gun.

The leader bent down. This is it! Slocum thought. He steeled himself for the knife thrust, hoping that the man would mercifully do it fast. But the Apache had only wanted to unbuckle Slocum's gun belt. He reached underneath, unbuckled it, and jerked it out. Then he buckled it on himself and looked at his reflection in the still little pool where Slocum had bent to drink.

"Ah," he said, contentedly. He spoke in Apache next. Slocum could get along in it. It was a very difficult language to learn, but he had picked up quite a lot of it in his years of wandering through Arizona and Mexico. "Make a fire," the Apache said. "A small one."

It was the end for him, Slocum knew.

## 2

An attempt to rob the Cattlemen's Bank in Tucson had failed. His two helpers were dead, and Slocum had been riding hard all the previous day, most of the night, and all morning. He had left without a thing except the Colt he was wearing. His Winchester was inside the bank, and the saddlebags were empty. A teller had wrenched the carbine from Slocum's grip when his attention had been distracted by a shot from the open window. He had made it out the back door, run through the alley, and gotten on his horse all right. He was sure that someone had betrayed him. He did not risk going back to the fleabag where he had been staying to pick up his bedroll and slicker. He knew that he would have to stay out of Arizona Territory for a year or two.

And then he had run into this little war party of Chiricahuas! Slocum turned his head. A young boy of fourteen or so was busily gathering little dried branches of pinyon, which grew thickly because of the abundant water. He was on his apprenticeship raid and had to do all the dirty work of the camp. The boy piled the twigs in a mound the size of two fists held together. The wood was directly under a strong horizontal pinyon branch. Slocum knew what that meant. The boy took a metal cylinder from his pouch and unscrewed the top. He withdrew a kitchen match and struck it across the corrugated base until it flared up. The twigs caught fire immediately.

Slocum knew what all that was for. He would hang head downwards from the pinyon, with his skull only a couple of inches from the fire. The Chiricahuas knew very well that the hottest part of a fire is not the flame itself but the air just above the flame. The Chiricahua Apaches—those closest to Mexico—had been fighting the Spaniards since they had first penetrated into Apacheria over three hundred years before. Then the Americans had come. No quarter had been given by either side. No other people in the Americas—and indeed, nowhere else in the world—had fought so long and so ruthlessly against the invader and been so mercilessly slaughtered. The survivors, in revenge, had developed torture into a fine art.

"Bring him to the tree," the leader said.

Slocum knew that they would tie his hands together behind his back as soon as they were released from the plank. He knew that his only hope was to try to escape as soon as the arrowheads were pulled from his hands. With that in mind, he embarked upon a plot designed to lure the Chiricahuas into a sense of contemptuous security. As the men approached him, the boy followed with a strip of rawhide. Slocum screamed in a perfect imitation of uncontrollable terror.

"Woman!" one of the men said in a disgusted tone.

Slocum flung his head rapidly left and right, opened his mouth, rolled his eyes upward, and stiffened. He thought that it was a pretty good imitation of a hysterical fainting seizure, and so did his captors. The man at Slocum's right wore a sheath knife on his left hip. It would be easy to grab it with his right hand when the man bent down. First he intended to trip the man to his left, wrench the knife out of its sheath, and then shove it in to the hilt. Two down. Next step, run three long paces to his chestnut, mount, lie flat on its back as protection against the immediate storm of arrows, and dig in the spurs. With any luck he might make it, especially since the Chiricahua were not mounted.

The alternative was to roast slowly. He did not think that he could handle the pain while his scalp was sizzling.

The two men bent down and snapped the reed arrow shafts. Then they pulled Slocum's transfixed palms straight up. The pain was savage, but in his years as a cavalry captain for the Confederacy and in the years that followed as he roamed the West, Slocum had been no stranger to pain. All that was required was to make his mind go away.

He lay inert, faking unconsciousness. The time to make his move would come when they had pulled him to his feet. That would put him close to each man. As soon as they pulled him erect, Slocum burst into movement. He thrust his left leg in front of the man at his left and clapped the man's back. The impact was so surprisingly agonizing to his ripped palm that he let out an involuntary cry of "Shit!" The Apache sprawled headlong. The man's face went into a cholla cactus.

"Ayee!" he shrieked, and clawed at his face.

Slocum had tried to clamp his right hand around the knife handle, but his hand and arm muscles could not obey. His ruined palm could not make the necessary gripping action. By then it was too late. The Apache kneed him in the groin, and Slocum bent over in agony. The man he had thrust headlong into the cholla struggled to his feet. He grabbed a stone the size of his fist and smashed it against Slocum's head. This time Slocum passed out for real.

## 3

When Slocum came to for a moment, he did not know where he was. Then he knew that he was upside down. There was a strange acrid smell in the air. His head felt extraordinarily hot; his face felt flushed. The heat reminded him of the malaria he had picked up on the Tampico coast, where he had been running guns for a revolution. The heat grew more intense. The pain struck his consciousness; the smell was that of his burning hair. They must have just hung him from the branch. The heat had awakened him. His hands were tied tightly behind his back. He saw several upside-down faces watching him with grave interest. The pain was very bad. It would get worse, he knew. The important thing was to be strong enough not to scream while he was dying. The Chiricahua would see that he was not a woman.

"Soldiers!" shouted the apprentice.

He was sitting high above them on the slope above the trail. One man kicked out the fire; another man cut the rawhide rope suspending Slocum, causing him to crash head first onto the still-burning wood. Two Apaches threw him without ceremony across the saddle of his horse. They lashed his wrists to one stirrup and his ankles to the other. They moved quickly and without panic. Slocum knew that his temporary reprieve meant only that he would be saved for slow torture at some isolated Apache *rancheria,* well hidden in a remote valley. He would slow down the war party, but no matter; the man with the cholla spines in his face would enjoy his revenge. He took the reins, and the group moved up the trail at a fast trot.

"I know that officer," the leader said. "That is their major. Look, he rides like a sack of corn. He looks like a fat blue pig sitting on a sack of corn."

The apprentice made himself look fat and bloated by collapsing upon himself. Then he jogged up and down in place with a miserably unhappy expression. The Apaches roared with laughter.

"Is there a scout?" the leader asked sharply. "Stop clowning!"

"There is no scout, Nachodise."

"Good," Nachodise said. He was satisfied. He pointed to the left, where a long, dried-up arroyo headed up farther into the mountains. "They won't see our trail go up the arroyo. You stay back of us," he said to the boy. "If the horse kicks stones out of place, you put them back. We'll have plenty of time for white eyes. Yes, plenty of time."

Dzildeh's knife flashed twice, slicing the rawhide thongs. Slocum slid head first onto the stony ground. His wrists were still tightly bound behind his back. His head banged against a sharp pebble. He let out a grunt of agony and then remained silent. Nachodise kicked him in the ribs, bent down, grabbed his faded green flannel shirt, and pulled him onto his back.

After four hours lashed face downward on a saddle, it was sheer ecstasy to lie on his back, taking the weight off his bruised, aching stomach. Faces gathered around and stared down at him. Slocum turned and slowly scanned the group. He counted carefully. There were twenty-two, all told: six fully grown men, three boys—one of them Dzildeh, the apprentice—and the rest women and children. He saw three married women. He knew that because their hair hung loose to their shoulders. There were four virgins. Their hair was arranged in a sort of ponytail; then the hair was folded up, then folded down. Both folds were tied together with a hairbow. Several very young children clung to their mothers. Slocum did not think it was a friendly gathering.

He was in a small grassy cleft pinned between two tall red cliffs. He judged the valley to be about two hundred feet wide. It was covered with grasses. Several *wickiups*—rude brush structures—were scattered about. It was the kind of place a man could never find unless he knew exactly where to look. It was an ideal hiding place. A narrow little creek hissed along the base of the western cliff. By the gnawed bones and trampled grass, Slocum estimated that the little band had been camped there about two weeks.

Nachodise stood over Slocum. He bent down and unbuckled his belt. He unbuttoned the trousers and jerked them down to the knees. He grabbed the waistband of Slocum's underdrawers and jerked

14  JAKE LOGAN

that down to his knees as well. A small boy trotted up with two fist-sized stones and handed them to Nachodise. Slocum knew what that meant.

Once, in the Superstition Mountains, he had come across a prospector who was screaming and writhing in agony. The man was naked. His voice had gone hoarse. He was holding his smashed testicles and rocking his torso back and forth. "Kill me," he had moaned, "kill me!"

Slocum had put him out of his misery with one bullet to the brain. The result of crushed testicles was several hours of excruciating agony followed by death. There were no survivors of that kind of trauma.

And now it was going to happen to him. Slocum had come very close to dying many times in the years since he had come back to his ancestral plantation at the end of the war and found his mother dying of pneumonia because a Yankee officer had taken all the quilts on a cold winter night and burned the magnificent old columned house. Slocum had traced the bluebelly up to New York State when the war was over. He had called the man out on his porch and then killed him. There were witnesses.

Slocum had fled to the frontier. And now, after all those years—the rustling, the bank robberies, the train heists—he was to die in a terrible manner. For the first time in his life he felt terror. Adrenaline spurted into his bloodstream. Only that morning he had eaten well: three eggs, a steak, and two cups of coffee. He still had enough strength to make a run for it if he could only get his legs free. They'd have to bring him down with a couple of arrows or even a lucky shot from his own Colt. If so, he would welcome that as a decent alternative. He could well imagine what crushing his testicles might be like; a simple kick to his balls had made him double over in agony and puke all over his pants.

No good. The rawhide was too tight. Too many people surrounded him. He would try to infuriate Nachodise. Maybe the Apache would knife him in his rage. He summoned his memory of Apache curses.

"Dog fucker!" he said.

Several women tittered.

Nachodise's face flushed red. His hand went to his knife hilt. Then he understood Slocum's intention. His hand dropped away. He shook his head and smiled. He squatted in front of Slocum and picked up the two stones, banged them together in Slocum's face, and grinned.

An old woman limped swiftly out of the crowd. She grabbed Nachodise's shirt and jerked it roughly backward. He fell on his rear end. A titter went up. It was clear that he was not popular, and that fact gave Slocum some small comfort.

"I want him," she said simply.

"Kazshe, go away!" Nachodise got up. "You are a crazy old woman!"

"Be quiet! I used to spank you, many times. Have you forgotten?"

The titters grew louder.

"He is my prisoner. I took him," Nachodise said sullenly.

"No matter," Kazshe replied calmly. "My husband and son were killed on that trip you took to Casas Grandes. Have you forgotten?"

Slocum remembered that two years before, thirty-two Apache warriors had been killed by a cleverly planned ruse down in Old Mexico. General Palacios had invited several bands of Chiricahua and Lipan Apaches to come to Casas Grandes for a peace talk. He had promised them broiled calf ribs and all the whiskey they could drink. Over eighty Apache warriors had come. When they were drunk, soldiers hidden in the adobe houses surrounding the plaza fired volley after volley into the drunken heaps. Only seventeen men escaped.

"I have not forgotten. I have killed many Mexicans since."

"That is very well. I want this American."

"But—"

Kazshe held up her hand. "I am getting old," she said. "I have no one to hunt for me. Since I broke my ankle, it is too hard for me to walk, to carry water, to build a *wickiup*. I want him."

"But Kazshe! He is too old! He will run away as soon as he can! You are a foolish old woman."

Kazshe swung a good roundhouse slap. She hit the man's face with all the force of her stocky build. He went over ass-backwards, and the crowd roared with laughter.

Nachodise realized that this was a battle he could never win. He got up and glared at her. He threw down the stones. "Take him! He will kill you one day and tear off your scalp and collect a bounty from the Mexicans, you stupid cow!"

He turned abruptly and shouldered his way angrily through the crowd. Kazshe stood over Slocum. Someone gave her a knife, and she sliced the rawhide thongs that held his wrists together. He sat up groggily and reached down to pull up his underdrawers and pants. But his hands were puffy around the arrow holes, and the tight clamp of the rawhide had cut off all circulation. His hands were as weak as a baby's.

The crowd drifted away to return to their occupations. Only a naked three-year-old remained. She stared at him with huge black eyes, with her thumb in her mouth.

"Stand up," Kazshe said in Apache. Slocum did not move. "Stand up!" she repeated. "Stand up, Slocum!"

Slocum stared at her as she motioned impatiently. He stood up, lost in wonder. How did she know his name? She pulled up his underdrawers and then his pants and buckled them.

As she worked, she talked in Apache. "I know you talk our language. You bought an Apache girl four years ago in Mexico. The Mexican soldiers had found a *rancheria* near Huachinera. They killed everyone and were going to rape her. You and four of your men heard the shooting. You were stealing cattle. You rode over. You took the girl from them. There was more killing. This time you did the killing. You killed four of them. The others ran away. Then you had to ride fast into Arizona. You had to leave the cattle behind because more soldiers were coming. Is this true?"

Slocum nodded. He regretted losing the five hundred head, and his men were angry with him for risking everything just to save an Apache girl. They had come back across the border with nothing to show for the time they had spent down there except empty bellies and exhausted horses. Slocum was not popular in those quarters for quite a while after that.

"She lived with you for a year. She told me that she taught you the language of the People."

"It is a very hard language."

"She told me you learned it fast, in the best place where a woman can teach a man."

Slocum smiled. Beds were always the best schoolrooms. "Saqu'o'la wanted to go back to her people," he said. "Is she here?"

"White soldiers killed her," Kazshe said, without anger.

Slocum did not know what to say. After a while she asked, "Will you stay and help an old woman?"

Slocum was silent.

"For a while, then?"

How long was a while? Slocum said to himself that a while would be until his wounds healed. That would be a month. She had saved his life. He owed her that much. He could spend a month knocking down pinyon nuts with a long stick. Later, when he had left, he could always send her something she could use: clothes, beads, anything.

"Yes," Slocum said finally. "A while."

"It is good," Kazshe announced with a smile.

His hands had turned red and puffy. Around the entrance and exit wounds they were throbbing painfully. Infection had set in. If there was anything an Apache *rancheria* didn't have, it was iodine, cotton, and gauze.

Kazshe patted the ground beside her in her *wickiup*. Slocum sat down and extended his hands for her inspection. "Umm," she said. Her palms were calloused, completely unlike his mother's. They turned his hands over very gently during her inspection.

"Wait," she said. When she had gone, Slocum lay back on the smoky, greasy buckskin that served as a rug. In spite of the throbbing jolts of pain in his hands and the dull ache on his raw skull, he fell asleep immediately. He was exhausted.

He woke up and saw Kazshe sitting beside a

small fire. Over it she had suspended a small kettle with an inch of water on the bottom. A pungent, acrid, pleasant smell came from it. She was boiling leaves. Slocum knew a lot about the vegetation of Arizona, but he did not recognize those long, lance-shaped leaves with jagged edges and an olive-green tinge. He knew that they must have come from some obscure little shrub he had never noticed.

When the water had turned the same color as the leaves, Kazshe reached in and grabbed a handful of the soggy leaves. She cried out because of the heat, and then she clapped the wet leaves on the back of Slocum's right hand. She applied the same poultice to the palm of that hand. She bound it firmly into place with a length of rawhide. She repeated the process with his other hand. Then she cut the hair around his burnt scalp with a sharp knife until only fuzz remained. She covered the burn with her poultice and tied it on with a dirty handkerchief under his chin. Within five minutes Slocum felt the pain begin to recede. He lifted his hands and stared at them. No iodine, no cotton, no sterile gauze—and a surgeon with dirt-encrusted hands! Yet Slocum knew that he would be fine in the morning. He fell asleep again.

## 4

Early the next morning, while the sky was just beginning to turn pink on top of the eastern ridge, hands gripped Slocum's shoulder and shook him violently awake.

"Wake up, wake up!" she hissed. "No noise! Soldiers coming!"

Slocum sat up, still drugged with fatigue. The pain had diminished. His scalp throbbed, but not with the fevered pounding that signaled infection. She pulled on his boots for him. His hands were not yet strong enough to hold anything more than a spoon.

Like all Apaches on the move, everyone was ready. In five minutes everything had been dropped into buckskin bags. The children had been awakened. One or two who started to cry with indignation or fear had their faces slapped by their mothers; they quickly subsided into an aggrieved silence.

The older children bubbled with excitement. A very old grandmother had been placed on Slocum's horse.

A girl stood outside the entrance of Kazshe's *wickiup*. With her arms folded, she stared boldly at him. Then, like a good Apache girl, she dropped her eyes, but only for a moment. Something about her did not look very Apache, Slocum thought. She wore a blue velvet ankle-length dress, which, Slocum guessed, either had been traded from the Navajos or had been part of the loot from a lonely westbound covered wagon. The loose Apache boot was about her ankles. It could be pulled as high as the knees for protection in cactus country. It fit tightly around her small, narrow foot. His eyes traveled upward.

Someone outside called, "Dilchay?"

She half turned to answer. Slocum liked her name. Her voice was a soft, almost husky contralto. Slocum liked that, too. As she stood there half turned away from him, she presented her body's profile. She wore absolutely nothing under the blue velvet. Her breasts stood up boldly. He judged her to be a perfect thirty-six. Her nipple perched like a hard little cherry at the apex of her left breast. Her buttocks were firm and moved sinuously under the tight clasp of the velvet when she turned and looked again at Slocum. He felt a warmth beginning in his groin. He wanted her. It was very obvious to Dilchay. She smiled at him and took a deep breath. Her breasts swelled toward him. But then someone—her mother?—called out again more insistently. Dilchay moved away with the smooth gliding walk and perfect posture of an Indian woman. Slocum knew that Dilchay was deliberately exaggerating her walk to make her hips rotate. She was issuing an invitation.

"Go!" Kazshe said sharply. "Hurry up! Your mother wants you!"

"Who is she?" Slocum asked.

"My sister's second husband's stepdaughter," Kazshe said sourly. "She—" She stopped abruptly.

"Yes?"

"It is not good to speak evil."

And that was all Slocum could get out of Kazshe.

In the center of the meadow outside the *rancheria*, Nachodise stood, arms akimbo, pompously barking orders. He watched them assemble. Slocum noticed that the man stared avidly at Dilchay, who deliberately ignored him.

"Now!" he shouted. "Up to the ridge!"

"Did you think we would walk *down* the hill to the soldiers?" Kazshe demanded. "You make a lot of noise and no sense, like a bullfrog." She derisively made the deep, plucked guitar twang of a bullfrog deep in her throat. It sounded perfect. Several women laughed.

Nachodise choked with rage. He pretended to ignore her. He strode to the head of the group and waved his arm. "Now!" he said. "No noise!"

"*Glung, glung,*" went Kazshe.

Slocum found it hard not to laugh, but he managed to control himself. He did not fancy the leader of the band being angry with him. There were too many ways in which contrived accidents might happen to him. And who would grieve over a white captive who had been given as a reluctant gift to an old woman who did not have a powerful family to protect and avenge her?

The people moved quietly. Stones clinked underfoot. Clearly, they were used to this kind of sudden movement. Slocum was astonished to hear how silently they moved. The iron horseshoes had been removed from his chestnut and leather shoes put on his hooves to make sure that his movement would be as silent as possible. There was no ringing of the iron as usually happened. The Apaches had prepared for such a fast move by pulling off the shoes during the night. Slocum's respect for their fieldcraft went up a notch. The slow shuffling of their moccasin-clad feet and their soft voices could not carry more than a hundred yards.

Kazshe was limping painfully. Slocum followed closely. Suddenly a quickly muffled scream came from her. He saw a heavy, thick brown rope clinging to her left boot. It was a big diamondback, heading back to his den after a night's hunting. It had not found anything; Slocum could see that there was no bulge in its belly. That meant that the snake's poison sacs were full. His hands were useless.

With one fast jump, Slocum planted his left foot heavily on the rattler's tail. With his sharply pointed cowboy boot, he kicked the snake's head. The force of the kick ripped the snake's head loose. The curved white fangs remained embedded in the deerskin. The snake coiled rapidly and struck at Slocum's right leg, but Slocum felt only a sharp rapping blow against his skin. The snake coiled again, but a bowstring twanged back of him. The big diamondback's coils were transfixed by an arrow. The tail and the head lashed about wildly in agony.

"My brother," Kazshe said to the snake, "I am sorry. I beg your pardon." Slocum did not laugh. He knew that it was the Apache custom to do that, to prevent another rattler from coming to avenge its mate's death. Kazshe pulled down her boot.

The yellow venom slid down inside the buckskin. Her skin was not broken. "You see, Slocum? I said I was sorry, and he was kind."

Maybe she has something there, Slocum thought. Who could say? Quietly the band moved upward.

The sentries had heard the cavalry patrol trying to move quietly in the predawn darkness. There was no way that could possibly be done with horses wearing iron horseshoes, and with cavalrymen covered with their accoutrements: rifles, sabers, iron stirrups, bouncing canteens, and bridles. Troops always jingled and clanked, thoroughly unlike Apaches on horseback. Apache horse gear consisted solely of rawhide thongs to control the horse. There were no stirrups. If a man had a pistol or a carbine or a knife, they were all kept separate so that none of them would bang against the others. There were no metal canteens to make noise. For a long ride across desert country, an Apache would kill a horse, gut it and fill the long intestines with water, and carry that coiled around his body. It made for a perfectly silent canteen that contained fifteen times more water than the U.S. Cavalry issue. And, of course, any horse stolen by them had its shoes pulled off and leather shoes bound on.

By the time the patrol reached the abandoned *rancheria*, the Apaches were over eleven hundred feet above them. They sat down and watched with amused interest while the soldiers set fire to the *wickiups*. Slocum thought that that was stupid. The loss of a *wickiup*—built in fifteen minutes or so—meant nothing to an Apache. It was a petty act of spite against a hard and ruthless enemy. Some innocent white settler would pay for that act. The Apaches believed in group responsibility. If a white man hurt an Apache, the Apache would hurt any white man, and so restore the earlier balance.

Nachodise reached into the buckskin bag he carried over his left shoulder. He pulled out a pair of officer's binoculars and stared through them down at the lower slopes. Nachodise had a hard face sawed into flat brown planes, as if an unskilled carpenter had been hacking away with a dull chisel at a slab of extraordinarily hard oak. His massive back muscles bunched under his dirty white cotton shirt as he swept the binoculars back and forth. He would be an ugly customer in a hand-to-hand fight, Slocum knew.

The soldiers were now boiling coffee for breakfast. The breeze brought the aroma to them. Slocum sniffed with longing. Nachodise was in a good mood that morning. He reached out with the binoculars.

"Do you want to look with the medicine glass?" he asked unexpectedly.

Slocum took them and scanned the valley. The light had gotten stronger. The black and brown dots in the valley suddenly were magnified into horses grazing.

"The white soldiers are stupid," Nachodise said.

"Some."

"That fat major with the blue eyes and the big brown mustache, down there by the fourth horse. His name is Murray. Do you know him?"

"No."

"We do. He wants to find us. He has been following us for three months. Each time we give him some empty *wickiups*. Then they burn them. Then they drink coffee."

It all seemed stupid to Slocum, but he said nothing.

Nachodise went on. "Every time some Apaches go down to Mexico and burn a wagon train or something, he comes to look for us. Even if we have been gathering pinyon nuts for the winter or shooting deer for jerky. So we move."

"But he finds you. He is not so stupid."

"This time he came close, yes. Maybe he knows where we are because someone here tells him. People think it is because of those Pima scouts he has."

Nachodise suddenly grinned as at a delicious recollection. It was the first time Slocum had seen him smile. He had large and very white teeth. They flashed in the dim light like the teeth of a great white shark Slocum had once seen in the Gulf of California as it rolled to seize a naked Indian swimming in the surf off Sinaloa.

"I caught one of those Pimas once. He lived for two days. He was very brave." Nachodise's smile vanished. He stared at Slocum and held out his big brown hand for the binoculars. "You would last ten minutes. Maybe not that. Your hands are better? Kazshe knows much about wounds. You are very lucky—very, very lucky."

Slocum was not going to argue with him whether he would last ten minutes or less. No man knows how much torture he can stand until he stands it. Nachodise may have been right. On the other hand, he may have been wrong. As long as Slocum did not have the use of his hands, he was not going to argue with anyone, especially a hard case like Nachodise.

"But how did the Pimas find us?" Nachodise went on. "Well, maybe Dilchay told them."

"Dilchay?" Slocum was startled.

"She is only half Apache. Her mother was taken

in Mexico. Her mother talked a lot to Dilchay about her people. Maybe Dilchay wants to go back. Maybe she lets the Pimas know where we are." He shrugged.

Now Slocum knew why Kazshe was so reluctant to talk about Dilchay.

"But she is beautiful! I want to fuck her," Nachodise said. "Then later I make her talk. I bet she'll scream too much, though. White people scream too much." He finished his speech with contempt.

Slocum was not going to argue the point. Nachodise looked down at the band's abandoned, smoking *rancheria*. He pointed to a tiny blue figure.

"That major," he said wistfully. "Oh, I would like him for half an hour. Oh, very much."

## 5

"Ah, Major. Good afternoon."

Major Murray's eyes were still narrowed against the fiery glare of the Tucson street outside. He stopped at the green baize door leading to the back room of the Goldminer's Daughter and waited a few seconds for his eyes to adjust to the darkness. Darkness was what people wanted after they had been facing the brilliant sun day after day in the desert west of Tucson or after they had withered under its pitiless light as they rode down from the Santa Ritas. And there were people there who did not care to be openly seen, such as Gompertz.

"You're Gompertz?" Murray asked.

"That's right."

Gompertz was well dressed in a black waistcoat and handmade boots. He was six feet tall and wore long sideburns and gray trousers. Across the front of his black vest ran a heavy gold watch chain. He pulled out his gold repeater and looked at it.

"On time," he grunted. "Good. I like that."

Murray had made a considerable effort to get to the Goldminer's Daughter on time. It was a very important talk for him. His bay mare was covered with foam as she stood panting at the hitching rack. He had ridden her hard.

"Where's Bailey?" Murray demanded.

"Glad you could come," Gompertz said. "Have a seat."

Gompertz waved a fragrant, expensive cigar at the chair beside him. Major Murray sat down with a grunt. He was twenty pounds overweight, and it was getting harder all the time to carry that extra poundage. His thighs filled his blue uniform pants till they looked like overstuffed sausages.

"*Where's* Bailey?" Murray asked again, this time with asperity.

"Our mutual friend thought it would be better to remain—shall we say—invisible?"

"What kind of bullshit talk is that?"

Gompertz looked pained. "Our mutual friend—I think it better not to name names in public places—thought it better for me to come and work out all the implications. I see what you're thinking: 'Will I have to deal with the messenger boy every time I want to discuss something with our mutual friend?' And the answer to that is yes. It is simple common sense. Our negotiations are rather delicate. They can be misunderstood, to put it mildly."

Murray sighed with vexation.

"Drink?" Gompertz asked.

"Sure," Murray said. He was slightly mollified.

Gompertz shoved a bottle of Old Tippecanoe across the table. It was the best bourbon in the world. The major warmed slightly. Gompertz shoved a glass after it. "I can't vouch for the glass," he said.

Murray liked liquor, and the tempestuous Mrs. Murray would not allow any in their quarters. He had been drinking too much lately, worrying about the lack of promotion and the possibility that he would be retiring on a major's half pay, a fate she had predicted and cursed. He filled his glass half full and drank it down in four gulps. Gompertz watched him sharply.

"Don't worry," Murray said. His tongue was thickening. "Tell Bailey I can handle it."

"I'm not so sure." He had checked out Murray's drinking.

"Well, be sure," Murray said sharply. Then he immediately added, "I beg your pardon." He needed Gompertz. Gompertz would pass on Murray's idea to Jason Bailey if he liked it. "I had a hard day in the field, and I'm getting a little too old to ride up and down mountain trails after those goddamn Apaches."

"Pardon accepted," Gompertz said smugly.

Murray wanted to kick his ass around the table, but he made his face pleasant instead. What was at stake here was Bailey's ability to make Murray President of the United States. Murray knew that Bailey was not only the richest man in Arizona Territory—he was also the Republican political boss. He chose the slate for each election. One more thing about him gave Murray his handle: Bailey was very, very greedy. He was the man who had first said, "Hell, I ain't greedy about ownin' land. I just want what touches mine."

"Nothing much to do these days," Murray said. "A man takes a drink out of sheer boredom."

"Can't say I blame you, with your Civil War record. Not many laurels to be won along Indian trails, are there?" Gompertz smiled and pulled on his cigar. He didn't want to offend Murray by remarking on the man's drinking. He thought a small warning that the major's drinking should be controlled would be taken by him as a hint from Bailey. Gompertz poured another glass to prove that there had been nothing personal in the remark. He was somewhat gratified to see the major sip it instead of gulping it down like the first one.

"Well?" Murray demanded.

"There's no need to rehash your record, Major. It's a very impressive one."

Indeed it was. Bailey had had Gompertz check it out thoroughly as soon as Murray hinted that he would like a meeting. Bob Edwards, the incumbent territorial governor, was a stupid nincompoop and a poor vote getter. Bailey had been looking around for someone else.

Murray came from Maplegrove, Michigan, which was just a wide place in the road. His father was a carpenter and an enthusiastic supporter of the Whig Party. He did a lot of traveling and talking for the local candidates and had become tax assessor for the county as a reward. When Murray was eighteen, his father's influence won the boy a West Point appointment. The year was 1859. When war broke out, the four-year course was shortened to three, and Murray, near the top of his class, chose the cavalry.

The young second lieutenant was slim in those days and rode well. The men liked him. His courage was magnificent. When it had become clear that the Southerners, with their rural background, were doing all the successful and attention-getting

SLOCUM AND THE MAD MAJOR 33

cavalry raiding, the Northern command looked around and saw this handsome, blond, colorful, and courageous second lieutenant. He had been making reconnaissance rides in and out of Southern-held Virginia. Old General Bascom felt that Murray was an up and coming lad, and in a month he had promoted him to a captaincy.

Bascom wrote a letter to a fellow West Pointer in the general staff. "I have a cavalry captain," he began. "Name is Murray, from Michigan. He has dash and fire, is courageous, intelligent. Has initiative; actually knows how to read maps. Thinks fast, very innovative. He's the first officer I've had in my command who's of same caliber as Jeb Stuart. We need someone like him to give the North some spirit. I think you ought to consider him in your long-range planning. Look into this."

At the War Department, General Yates put down the letter, made a note on his pad, called in his aide, and talked to him briefly. Then he put on his hat, called for his carriage, and was driven to the White House. He had picked up hemorrhoids during his years in the saddle, and so he rode in his carriage sitting on a feather-stuffed pillow. He sent in his card and was admitted immediately.

Lincoln respected the old general. Yates was approaching retirement and cared nothing for offended feelings along the chain of command. He was famous for speaking bluntly. This was the sort of attitude in the military that appealed enormously to Lincoln, who had very little respect for the military mind.

Yates walked painfully into the Oval Office with his pillow.

"Good morning, Mr. President."

"How are you, General?" Lincoln stood up, his

six-foot four-inch height unfolding like a carpenter's ruler snapping back and forth. "And how are your piles?"

"Mr. President," Yates said, sitting down delicately on his pillow, "try to imagine someone has some red-hot barbed wire. They are engaged in ramming it up your ass and turning it and shoving it back and forth at the same time. That's a little bit what it's like."

Lincoln chuckled. Now that he had had his laugh, business could begin. "Brother Yates," he said, "tell me what's on your mind."

General Yates did not waste time. "I have a young cavalry captain. He's made for fast, small raids. He brings back useful prisoners and information. He seems to be a forceful, strong commander. The men like him."

Lincoln laced his long, strong brown fingers together and waited patiently. He knew that Yates would not waste his time.

"Three days ago, in a hard downpour, he was riding by himself cross-country. He was wearing a rubber waterproof poncho over his uniform. On one of those back-country roads he came across twelve rebel ammunition wagons. They had an escort of fifteen troopers. He rode right up to the troop and demanded to know who was in charge."

Lincoln began to smile. Yates knew that the President liked stories like that. He lit a cigar in order to build suspense and then resumed his story:

" 'I am, by God!' Murry yelled. 'I'm Major Clum, on Stuart's staff, and I'll eat you for breakfast, you, sir, you insolent son of a bitch! I'll have your stripes for this!' "

Lincoln's small smile had widened till it became a wide, delighted grin.

## SLOCUM AND THE MAD MAJOR 35

The sergeant, Yates went on, said that he was Sergeant Wood.

" 'It may soon be Corporal Wood,' Murray said, glowering. 'Now tell me, where the hell are you going with those wagons?'

" 'To the valley. To Stonewall.'

" 'Stonewall *what*?' "

Yates said that the poor man had misunderstood. Murray now fell upon him like the wrath of God.

" 'Don't you think *I* know that the man's name is Jackson?' he roared. 'I repeat, Stonewall *what*?'

"The bewildered sergeant finally understood what he was driving at.

" 'Stonewall, sir.'

" 'That's better,' Murray said, with a petty air of satisfaction. He had the man bulldozed and under control. Then he began his strategic planning. 'Now,' he demanded, 'who among you is from this part of Virginia?' Murray had told Yates later that he placed their accents as being deep South, probably from a Mississippi brigade.

" 'No one, I reckon, sir,' said the sergeant.

" 'I thought so,' Murray said in a disgusted tone. 'You just keep going the way you're going, and you know what's going to happen? Well?'

" 'No, sir.'

" 'Well, I'll tell you,' Murray said with that air of pompous smugness achieved by almost all junior officers on a general's staff. 'You'll run right into a Yankee named Murray. He'll be down on those wagons like the whole Missouri on a sandbar.'

" 'But that's the way we was told to go!' said the sergeant. He held up a sketch map. Murray held out his hand and the sergeant dutifully handed it over. The map was a good one and accurate. Murray gave it a disgusted look. He held out a hand and barked, 'Pencil!' The sergeant didn't have one and got a black look from Murray. One of the privates fished out a stub and handed it over. Murray lifted his poncho and, placing the map on the saddle horn, crossed out the correct route and drew a new one, which would lead the ammunition wagons right into the middle of his command.

"*This* way!' he snapped and handed the map over. At that moment he almost had a heart attack as he realized that by lifting his poncho, he had exposed his blue uniform. But later he figured that the men were so terrorized that they refused to believe their eyes; he also said that if someone had made a remark about it, the terrible officer would have him court-martialed.

" 'Gosh, sir, thanks,' the sergeant said."

At this point in the story, Lincoln let out a great guffaw and slapped his thigh in huge delight. "And so we won a rebel ammunition train, thanks to this Captain Murray?"

"Yes, Mr. President."

"Has he been promoted?"

"Yes, sir."

"Good, good! Initiative and daring must be encouraged. I hope other young officers will take the hint. Now, Yates, I appreciate the story. But surely you didn't come here just to bring a little joy into my life."

"No, Mr. President."

"Go ahead, Yates. You have a twisted mind. I admire it."

"Mr. President, the South has Jeb Stuart. It has Morgan. It has McIntyre. It has fine, daring cavalry leaders. We have none. I think that the young man will provide—"

"I understand, friend Yates. We will give him a

good command, send reporters from the *Herald* and from the English papers to write up his exploits, send a good war artist, right?"

"I was thinking of making him a brigadier-general."

"How old is the lad?"

"Twenty-four."

"A bit young, Yates. I will have to face a great deal of angry criticism from high officers who have been passed over and from the newspapers."

"Yes, sir."

"But you think it's necessary."

"Sir, when you give a man responsibility, you have to give him rank. Rank will let him ask for good mounts. He can get good men and good equipment and the new repeating rifles. With these and with his proven abilities—"

"We will have a Northern Morgan, eh?"

"Precisely, Mr. President."

"Go to it, friend Yates! I'll back you."

General Yates stood up and reached for his pillow. Lincoln unfolded his long frame and stood at the window, looking into the garden.

"How did the young man vote?" Lincoln asked.

"Straight Republican, sir." Yates had taken the trouble to investigate Murray's background thoroughly. "Not only that, his father is tax assessor of the county. He worked hard for your election."

"All the better, all the better," Lincoln said with satisfaction. "That's something I can throw at them when the name-calling begins."

"Thank you, Mr. President."

"One thing more." The wan, tired, gaunt face broke out into a grin. That was something that always fascinated Yates—the way Lincoln's visage moved from the mask of tragedy to the mask of comedy.

"Sir?"

"Some day, when the war is over and we all have plenty of time, I should like to sit down with young Mr. Murray and hear that ammunition train story from his own lips. I would enjoy that!"

Brigadier General Murray got his promotion and his command. Within three months his name was a household word throughout the North. In one battle he had had three horses shot from under him. He had a charmed life. Men were killed all around him, but he was never wounded. The papers called him the "Boy General." When he went on home leave to Michigan, the town went wild. They had a big parade. There was a band, and flags were draped all up and down Walnut Street. He made a patriotic speech. Finally, Caroline Saxon, the daughter of the town banker, now decided that he was good enough material to marry. They took a two-week honeymoon and got along well enough, and then he went back to his command, feeling that he was king of the mountain and that everything was now for the best in the best of all possible worlds. Lincoln wrote to him, asking him to drop by whenever he might be in Washington, but then the fortunes of war took Murray into Tennessee. But Murray had decided that he would wait to see Lincoln during the victory parade in the capital so that he could ride in front beside Grant and Sherman.

He might have gotten his wish, with all the political consideration for the future that such a procession might have won for him, but for two things. One was, of course, the death of Lincoln months before the parade. The second problem was the death of Yates late in 1864. Without a strong backing in the War Department, the natural jealousy among high officers ensured that Murray would ride way at the end of the parade.

He had been brevetted a lieutenant general only for the duration of the war. As soon as it ended, he reverted back to a captain's rank and pay. The army was cut back to a skeleton force, no more than was necessary to patrol the frontier. America had no foreign enemies, and so there were no promotions. Caroline began to grow bitter. She missed the prestige, the status, the fine houses that they could live in when she came to visit him where he was in action. She missed the reporters and the stories they had written about the Boy General and his stunning red-headed wife, Caroline.

Twenty years on the frontier, facing naked savages usually armed only with lances or bows and arrows, was not the way to fame or fortune. Out of sheer boredom he took a Cheyenne mistress when he was stationed at Fort Riley in Kansas. In Dakota Territory he took an Ogalala Sioux girl. His wife found out and gave him a hard time. He loved her. He began to drink. He acquired a potbelly. His famous golden locks began to thin out. He took to wearing a hat almost all the time, although up to then he had been famous for going bare-headed. Caroline began to nag him because a major's pay was not enough to maintain a good house. She wanted a surrey; she wanted a piano.

Then, lately, he remembered his old dream of riding in the victory parade up there in 1865 beside Grant and Sherman and Sheridan. He had been thinking ahead. People would remember him for that, and in fifteen or twenty years, he could run for congressman from Michigan. Grant had made it; Sherman and Sheridan didn't care for the political life. Well, that made it all the better for him.

There he was, talking to Gompertz. Murray had made it a point to find out about Bailey's background. If Bailey was the man to ride on to the Presidency—who knew?—Murray wanted to know who he would be dealing with. Bailey was a crude, brilliant financier who had come to Arizona ten years before from Chicago. He had been swinging a maul in a slaughterhouse, killing cattle. One day, when he had figured out how much the cattle were bringing to the ranchers, he quit the job and went west. He wanted the action at both ends.

He bought a ticket to Flagstaff. There were ranches up there on the Mogollon Rim, a bit dangerous, maybe, with the White Mountain Apaches. But no one ever said that he didn't have guts. He became a night hawk. He could sit a horse without falling off, and the job of night horse herder didn't require much skill. In a few months, by keeping his mouth shut and watching a lot, he had picked up a lot of cow knowledge. In the fourth month he was promoted to a regular cowpuncher's job. He learned that trade quickly. Another two years, and the Lazy J took a chance on him as a foreman. He could handle the job and the men. He quietly filed his own brand at the county seat. He bought a couple of hundred acres from an Englishman who was sick of the Apaches and the hard winters up on the rim. Two hundred acres was a ridiculous size for a ranch, but not when it had rich grass and plenty of water. He began stocking the tiny JB ranch with stolen cattle. It was observed that many of his cows had two or even three calves, while cows on the neighboring Bar S Bar suddenly became barren and went around bawling their desire to have calves of their own. The man who had made that remark was shot in the back one night as he was mounting his horse outside Mattie Brown's cathouse in Prescott. Nothing could be proved.

Bailey shipped his cattle east. He did very well. He bought more land and more cattle. After ten years he owned twelve thousand acres on and below the Mogollon Rim. Occasionally he had some trouble with the White Mountain Apaches, but he was a hard and vindictive man. His ranch house was a fortress. He hired well-armed men who were as hard as himself. They had no compunction about following up Apache raids and killing all the Apaches they came across, whether they were peaceful or hostile. Bailey made a point of hiring men on the owl hoot trail—men who were fleeing sheriffs—and it became know that it was too risky for just about anyone, white man or Apache, to be found riding on or near his property.

His cows began acquiring children to such a degree that some of them had six or seven. Bailey soon realized that it would be smart to have the law on his side. He financed the election of sheriffs in his county and in the two neighboring counties as well. This paid off. Complaints got mislaid, lost, or postponed. Warrants couldn't be served. He helped Edwards get appointed as territorial governor. He entertained traveling senators at his ranch house, which he had expanded until it had become the showplace of the rim.

When the army began building up its posts and forts in the territory, Bailey not only became the major supplier of beef to the Quartermaster Corps, he also furnished hay, beans, dried apples, and all the other things an army needs. He provided all the posts and forts in central and southern Arizona. The scrawny culls went to the army and the better stock to Chicago. He made a lot of money on both deals. He bribed army weighmasters to accept short weight. He even went to Washington and spread money around in the Senate Committee of Military Appropriations.

When a few honest quartermasters began to file complaints with the Army Department about wet hay being delivered for dry weight, pebbles in the sacks of beans, rat-infested flour, and all the other little tricks that Bailey had no compunction about using, those quartermasters suddenly found themselves transferred to Oregon or Florida. In places like that, without Indian warfare, their chances for promotion were reduced to zero. It was a complex and foolproof organization he had constructed.

Murray knew a lot about it. He had come across the rotten beef and the damp hay. But he knew that Bailey had protection in high places. While wondering what to do about it, he had suddenly decided not to fight Bailey with his ineffective weapons but to join him and use him. He knew that Bailey would want to know what would be in it for him. What Murray would do would be simple and effective: He would make sure that the Apaches were forced into constant open warfare. More troops would be called to the frontier. Huge amounts of grain and beef would be needed. Wagon trains would be needed to carry all the vast supplies to the forts. Millions would be made; and all of it would go into Bailey's greedy hands. Murray knew how to hold the cornucopia of plenty, and he could pour it into Bailey's hands. All he wanted in return was the assurance of Bailey's intensive political and, if need be, financial backing. Compared to what Bailey would be raking in on the quartermaster contracts, it would be a drop in the bucket.

"All right, Gompertz," Murray said heavily. "Listen carefully."

# 6

Slocum woke up. The night had become warmer because of a wind blowing up from Mexico. Everyone was asleep except the sentinels on watch far down the mountain. He threw aside the buckskin blanket. He was thirsty, and there was no water in the small clay jar. He got up quietly and walked out. When Slocum wanted to, he could move as quietly as an Apache. Once outside, he walked across the meadow filled with knee-high owl clover and poppies. A narrow creek bubbled along at the base of a jagged peak that seemed to snarl at the sky like a vicious animal.

This was a harsh and beautiful land. It had none of the soft, almost feminine beauty of his native Mississippi. He had not been home since the Civil War had ended. It was still too risky to go back. Now, looking up at the moon pinned against the jagged peak and feeling the warm wind blowing gently against his face, Slocum felt sure that he did not want to go back. This country held enough beauty for him.

He lay flat on the clover and bent his head to drink. The water was ice cold, and he drank his fill. As he lifted his head, he saw Dilchay sitting on a flat rock on the other side of the creek. Her knees were drawn up under her chin, and her arms clasped her legs.

"Ayeee! You were very thirsty!"

He wiped his mouth and looked at her.

"What will you do when you are well?"

That question had occurred to Slocum many times. He had no money. The gang he had put together with such patience for the bank heist must have scattered like quail when the attempt blew up in their faces. He had seen Jeff Brinton and Tom Howard go down, riddled by bullets. The other three had known that they were to meet at Naylor's Crossroads, a few miles north of Flagstaff, if things went badly. The scattering was Slocum's idea. He had copied it from the Apaches, who created so many trails for any pursuing party that the trailers usually gave up in disgust.

But that one week had come and gone over three weeks ago. If any of the survivors had made it to Naylor's Crossroads, they would be sure that Slocum had been killed. As a result, Slocum knew, they had drifted all over the West. It would take months to find them, put together a team, and work out a new plan.

"When I am well," Slocum said, "I will become an Apache warrior."

"You are joking?" she said angrily.

Indeed, he had made the remark as a joke, but immediately afterward, he came to regard it as not a bad idea at all. At least he would have food, lodging, and protection from the group. As for being a warrior, he was in fine physical condition, except for his hands. Three or four more weeks would take care of that. He could run long distances. He was a superb shot. Most Apaches were no good with guns because ammunition was too expensive to waste at practice.

"You couldn't even hit that rabbit yesterday!"

He had drawn a bow to aim it at a tree trunk. A rabbit suddenly sat up beside the tree. Slocum swung the bow, pulled and released the arrow. Two things happened immediately: The immensely powerful shock of the suddenly released bowstring tore the bow from his still-feeble hands, and the rabbit contemptuously did not move. The arrow missed him by three feet.

"Ayee, you looked so stupid!"

She shook her hood. The gesture made her long, glossy black hair sway back and forth. She wore it loose, like the married women. In the shadow of her deerskin skirt he stared at the long length of her brown thighs. She wore a purple velvet blouse. It had once been a long gown for an officer's wife whose scalp now decorated a Sioux lance. The dress had been traded southward to Apache country. The blouse now had buttons shaped by Navajo silversmiths out of dimes. It buttoned down the front, and it had been cut at the waistline. It had been made for a much smaller woman than Dilchay, whose breasts filled it to bursting. Her nipples stretched the fabric even more. They looked like marbles under the smooth fabric.

Dilchay knew very well that Slocum was staring hungrily at her body. With a smile she unbuttoned the top two buttons. It had been over two months since Slocum had been with a woman, and the experience had been bad; she had cried afterward from guilt.

One good thing about Indian women, Slocum thought: They loved to screw, thought it as natural as eating, and wasted no time feeling guilty. One other thing about them: They were deadly when they became sexually jealous. Slocum had once spent a couple of months with an Arikara woman in an abandoned line camp in Montana, near the borders of the Crow country. He had never known anyone as silent as Tall Woman was: passionate as hell in bed, yet still silent. Once Slocum had spent a night in town with another woman. When he came back to the camp next afternoon and fell exhausted into bed beside her, she immediately smelled the stranger's perfume.

She got up and made the longest speech Slocum had ever heard her make since he had met her. She said, "You son of a bitch," grabbed his Colt from the holster, and fired six shots at him. They all missed because she was so mad.

Here there would be no problems with jealousy. Dilchay was far and away ahead of all the other women in looks. He felt his penis begin to swell. She was aware of his heightened interest. She took a deep breath and let her breasts swell even farther against the velvet. His stare had aroused her as well. Her nipples had grown larger. Slocum stood up and waded across the stream. As soon as he stood next to her on the flat rock, she embraced his thighs, leaned close, and pressed her hot face against his penis. It swelled immediately. She mouthed its outline with her hot lips and then gently reached out and cupped his testicles. Slocum's heart speeded up. He slid a hand into her open blouse and cupped one brown breast in his palm. The blood-engorged nipple was round and hard as an olive. He rolled it gently between his fingers. She gasped with pleasure. Slocum knew that she would not play any game of advance and retreat.

She unbuttoned his fly and took out the hard length of his fully erect penis. She ran her wet, half-open mouth up and down the shaft. He unbuttoned her blouse all the way and pulled it off roughly. She helped him by pulling her arms out. Not once did she stop sliding her tongue along the engorged purple vein that ran along the base of his penis. It was almost too much. He pushed her face aside in order to regain control. He did not want it to end too quickly. She understood the gesture and waited patiently for his signal to continue.

Beside the rock was a thick mat of dried needles from the nearby pine trees. She pulled off his shirt, placed it flat under the soft, spongy fragrant surface, put her blouse and her skirt on it as well, lay down, and held out her arms. She was smiling. Slocum kicked off his pants and underdrawers and kneeled down. She put her arms around his waist, caressing his powerful back muscles. Then she took his penis into her mouth and used her fingers to gently stroke and caress his testicles. He was on the point of ejaculation when a massive weight crashed against his back and forced him on top of Dilchay.

For one horrible second Slocum thought that it was a grizzly, but the smell of human sweat and a muffled curse in Apache identified the aggressor as Nachodise. Slocum rolled to one side just as Nachodise aimed a hard kick at his face. He jerked his head to one side, and the big moccasin-clad foot brushed his face. The kick threw Nachodise off balance, and for a moment he stood balanced on one foot. Slocum grabbed an ankle and heaved upward. Nachodise crashed onto his back with a harsh grunt, rolled over with surprising speed for such a heavy man, and made a grab for Slocum's foot. His hands slid off Slocum's damp skin. Nachodise's extended arm gave Slocum the advantage he needed against the man's superior strength. He grabbed Nachodise's open palm and revolved the stiffened arm until the elbow locked; then he threw himself backward, with his thighs on either side of the Apache's arm. By pulling the stiffened arm across his crotch, he had acquired the necessary leverage to immobilize Nachodise.

When the Apache tried to move, Slocum pivoted the arm a fraction of an inch. Nachodise panted in agony and subsided.

"Move and I will break it," Slocum said. He remembered that this was the man who had tried to fry his brains. He moved the arm half an inch. The pain was enormous, yet Nachodise did nothing but take a deep breath. The man could take it as well as hand it out. Slocum respected that.

Nachodise suddenly heaved his body upward. It was no good. Slocum simply moved the arm half an inch. Nachodise stopped all movement and panted. It was a trick Slocum had picked up from a Chinese laundryman whose little shack he had saved from being dynamited by some drunken Irish miners near Virginia City.

"Do you surrender?"

Nachodise growled his assent. Slocum released him. Nachodise sat up and rubbed his shoulder, looking at Slocum with respect. It hurt because of the leverage Slocum had worked against it.

"I—" Nachodise began, and it was only because of Slocum's very fast reflexes that he was able to seize Dilchay's wrist as she plunged past him with Nachodise's big knife in her upraised hand. The Apache's back was to her. If it had not been for Slocum, Dilchay would have buried the knife to the hilt in Nachodise's back. Slocum stuck the knife in his belt and held the naked, screaming girl at arm's length.

Nachodise's dark, glowering face broke into a smile. She had fallen to her knees in her rage after Slocum had taken the knife from her. She was scooping up handfuls of pine needles and throwing them with both hands at Nachodise. The air was filled with clouds of needles and dust.

"Son of a Mexican!" she yelled. "Snake! Burro!"

The laughter of the men infuriated her even more, and she cursed until her voice grew hoarse. Finally she fell silent. She was glistening with sweat and covered with needles. Little rivulets of sweat made tracks between her breasts and down her flat brown stomach.

"Go in the creek and wash up," Slocum ordered. She did so obediently, and he handed the knife back to Nachodise.

"That was a good trick you did with my arm," the Apache said in frank admiration. "Show me how you did it."

"It is my medicine."

"Will you sell it to me?"

"Maybe. Not now."

Nachodise nodded. He understood that it was a secret power, not to be divulged casually.

"Will you sell it to me soon?"

"Probably not," Slocum said pleasantly.

Nachodise nodded again. "We are even," he said,

and walked away. Slocum watched him. He was not so sure.

"Come lie down," Dilchay said.

His hands hurt badly from their hard use. "Not now," he said. They dressed silently and walked back.

# 7

Kazshe had made a meat-drying rack out of several small branches resting upon four forked sticks. She was cutting venison into narrow strips. The heat and the breeze at that height would dry them quickly.

"Ah, look!" she called out suddenly. "The seven black rattlesnakes!" Slocum was startled and looked. She was pointing at some black writhing thunderclouds approaching the mountain. "See them fight one another!" she said.

The black clouds were tumbling; Slocum could imagine them as snakes.

"And look! One of them is biting the earth!" A jagged streak of lightning struck the peak. "Rattlesnakes are good to us," she said. "They take messages to the gods who live under the earth. They warn us not to step on them. You must be good to them," she said severely.

Slocum smiled and promised. The storm went as quickly as it had come.

He was happy and relaxed and proud of himself. He had killed his first deer early that morning with an arrow. He had hunted on the ridge because he knew that the cold air, descending, would bring his scent down to the trail used by deer. Instead, he waited on the lower side of the trail, and sure enough, an unsuspicious buck came along. It had taken him all morning to cut it up and bring it back to the *rancheria*. The band was not using the few guns it possessed, since a shot might attract the attention of enemies, particularly Murray's Pima scouts, who were always patrolling like restless wasps against their hereditary antagonists.

When Slocum had drawn the bow, he realized that his hands had healed completely. For the first time, he was able to repay Kazshe for everything she had done for him. Most of the men were off on a hunting trip to the east, where a herd of deer had been spotted yesterday afternoon. Two boys had been assigned the job of sentinels while the men were gone.

Nearby, sitting cross-legged on the ground, Dilchay was cracking pinyon nuts and dropping the kernels into a small Papago basket woven with a deer design. She sensed his gaze and turned. She had been angry at him since he had stopped her from knifing Nachodise two weeks before. She brushed her long black hair from her flushed face with the back of her brown hand. She stared back at him, frowning. Suddenly she smiled. She pointed to the flat rock where they had started to make love, and she called out one word: "Tonight." Slocum's heart jumped. She had forgiven him.

\* \* \*

Up on the ridge trail the two sentinels were bored. They had scanned the valley and the trails below in a perfunctory fashion but had seen nothing of interest. They yawned and slid down the slope to a more comfortable, level area and began playing the knucklebone game. The gambling became hot and heavy. One boy lost his moccasins and then his knife. All their attention was focussed on the bones. They did not see the two Pima scouts who were slowly easing up the ridge behind them.

When the men finally got into position, one slowly raised his head behind a clump of *sacaton*. The boys were fifteen feet below them, completely absorbed in the game. One scout nudged the other. They rose slowly to their feet, their knives held at the ready. The leader nodded sharply, and the Pimas launched themselves at the unsuspecting boys. When they had finished, one scout took off his shirt and waved it back and forth. Major Murray, flat on his belly across the valley, just below the neighboring ridge, saw the flutter of the shirt. He grunted with satisfaction.

"Sibley!" he called out.

The man beside him turned his head and looked at Murray. Captain Sibley did not like Murray but was careful to conceal his feelings. He was a man running to fat, like Murray, but he was only thirty-three years old. Since he was four inches taller, it did not look so bad on him.

"That's the signal!" Murray was exuberant. "They've taken out the sentries! Now tell me what your orders are. Be sure you get them right."

Sibley cursed silently. He did not like being treated like a brand-new second lieutenant.

"Yes, sir," he said stiffly. "I take my company. We go on foot. We leave our sabers behind. Also canteens. No noise. We spread out ten feet apart. We walk down the slope, across the valley, and up the ridge. Behind the ridge is the camp." He fell silent.

"And then?" Murray prompted.

"And then we kill them all."

"All?"

"All."

"Define 'all,' Captain."

This man is out of his mind, Sibley thought helplessly.

"All means every single goddamn Apache we come across in the camp."

"Good, good. Why are we doing that?"

"Because, as you said, 'Nits breed lice.'"

"Good. You just remember, and be sure you tell your men just what the Chiricahua do to our boys when they take them prisoner! I want to see them breathing fire when we hit the camp! Is that clear, Captain? I want to see more enthusiasm in your so-called leadership today. Do you understand, Sibley?"

"Yes, sir."

"Then hop to it."

Sibley stood up. His company was all dismounted. "Horseholders!" he called out, still angry as he thought about Murray's attitude. The change in the man was puzzling. Was it an effect of his heavy drinking? He shook his head. He had to attend to business; now was not the time to think about anything except the dirty business at hand.

One out of every three troopers was a horseholder. It was his job to hold his own and three other horses if a dismounted approach was called for. The men were all lying flat behind the ridge.

"No smoking there!" Sibley called out sharply.

He had just seen a man pulling a pipe out of his pocket. It was Corporal Morrissey, a persistent troublemaker who frequently had to be broken back into the ranks.

"Ain't smokin', Captain; just holdin' it in me teeth!"

"Put it back!"

Morrissey replaced it grumpily. Smoke might drift across and be smelled by the Apaches.

"Lieutenant."

Lieutenant Carter ambled up. He was an eager, alert, smiling blue-eyed lad of twenty-one, just out of West Point. His hair was very closely cropped in an unskillful attempt to emulate Murray. Murray was balding and wanted to make the bald spot less noticeable. Sibley had pegged Carter for an accomplished ass kisser almost from the first day he had stepped off the mail ambulance. He had seen nothing since to make him change his mind.

"The horses stay here, Carter," Sibley said crisply, trying to keep the dislike out of his voice. "Sabers off. No canteens. Walk down the line and make them take off anything which might rattle."

"Yes, sir."

Lieutenant Carter had never had a shot fired at him. A bullet fired at someone twenty feet away from a spur of Piccacho Peak had spanged against a rock thirty feet away from him. He had embroidered upon that casual event in a letter home to his mother in West Hartford. He enjoyed describing how the wind of the bullet had almost blown off his hat. But now he was beginning to feel that a lazily haphazard shot that hadn't even been aimed at him was a far different thing from walking into an Apache camp that surely was full of brutally savage Chiricahuas. He hoped that he would not disgrace himself by wincing at gunfire or vomiting or giving a wrong order in the heat of battle and having the men laugh at him.

"And when you finish with that," Sibley went on with distaste, "tell your men what these Chiricahuas do with prisoners. Tell them what the women do to them. Tell them what they do with the men's pricks."

Carter stared at him in astonishment. He had never thought that Sibley would say such things.

"The major's orders," Sibley said drily.

"Ah!" Carter said, nodding. It was an order, and by God, he would do a bang-up job of description. He turned and walked toward his platoon.

Sibley was a man of long experience. Like Murray, he had fought in the Civil War, but luck had been against him. In the second month of the war his detachment had blundered into a very strong cavalry force commanded by the formidable Morgan. Sibley, a brand-new lieutenant, had been wounded and left for dead. The rest of his detachment had retreated successfully. When he regained consciousness, he was in a Confederate field hospital. He spent the rest of the war in Andersonville Prison. In 1869 he was promoted finally to captain because of a brief skirmish against the Cheyenne in Kansas. Since then he was frozen into a captaincy. Retirement was not far off, and a captain's pension was pitifully small. If he played his cards right and did not antagonize his superior, he might retire as a major.

Sibley had no confidence in Carter's ability to handle the nasty detail that had been lined up for him. There would be no way he could see his platoon in action, spread out as they would be after the climb; the situation would get worse because of the haphazard arrangement of the *wickiups*. Then it would be every man for himself.

The horseholders, relieved that they would not be required for the advance, were sitting on the ground and holding the reins. Sibley looked at them sourly. He had some good sergeants in the company. They drank too much, however. They spent a lot of time in the guardhouse, but they were hard men and reliable in battle.

"Schultz!" Sibley called.

Sergeant Schultz came up and saluted crisply. "Sir?" He still retained a faint German accent. Schultz was tall and gaunt, with long freckled wrists that always stuck out from his sleeves. He spoke very little and had a beer belly. But he had a punch like a piledriver, as the men who were foolish enough to invite him to have it out back of the post trader's had found out. The men respected him.

"Watch young Mr. Carter," Sibley said quietly.

"Sure. You bet, Captain."

"All right, then. I think we can go. Keep them quiet. No shooting till I say so, or if we're shot at. You told 'em what Apaches do to prisoners?"

"Oh, you bet, Captain. They didn't like the rawhide especially."

Sometimes the Chiricahua took people they disliked strongly and tied a piece of wet rawhide around the base of the scrotum. They tied another thong, just as wet, around the root of the penis. They tied the man to a post in the open sun. As the rawhide dried in the heat, it shrank and became hard. In three or four days, the penis and the scrotum turned black. The man received plenty of food and water. Additional zest was supplied by the small sticks that were banged upon the testicles hour after hour. The agony was intense. On the fourth day one strong jerk would remove the necrosed penis and scrotum.

The line of dismounted cavalrymen moved down the slope and then across the narrow valley and up the opposite slope. The Pima scouts signaled them on; the *rancheria* still did not know that anything was wrong. Murray walked behind the line of skirmishers. He was no coward. He wanted to stay there to keep an eye upon everything. He was out of condition and had begun to puff with the exertion of the climb through the sagebrush and cactus.

When they were halfway up the slope, the grinning Pimas met them. A bloody scalp swung at each belt. Carter paled and then resolutely averted his eyes. The Pimas walked through the skirmishers. The men moved aside to let them pass, staring at the still-dripping scalps with fascinated disgust. Sibley was in charge of the Pimas. The scouts could communicate with the soldiers only in Spanish. Sibley spoke Spanish well.

"*No hay mucha gente en la rancheria,*" said one Pima. "There are few people in the rancheria."

"*Hay hombres, guerreros?* Are there any men? Warriors?"

"*Solamente los viejos.* Only old ones."

Sibley let out a sigh. Lieutenant Carter would not be tested in battle today. The Pimas said that there was a pretty little meadow, much grass, and plenty of water. Lots of big boulders were jammed together past the camp. Good place atop them for a sentry. But there was no sentry there. The Apaches had become careless. There were twelve *wickiups*. Sibley calculated silently that that meant there would be about sixty people down there.

"*Bueno,*" Sibley said to the Pimas. "*Puede andar.*

You can go." The Pimas would be useless for a month. Their religion made them withdraw from their group after a killing and sit for a month so that the ghosts of the slain would not come and bother the killers' relatives. After a month they would screw their wives, go to the fort, draw their rations, and give them to their families. Then they would cheerfully go off and kill more Apaches. It was a weird way of going to war. As Sibley climbed the hill, puffing slightly, he amused himself with thinking how the Civil War might have turned out should everyone have gone home on a month's leave after shooting or bayonetting an enemy. The morale would have been much better, but the only definite result would have been a very high birthrate.

He looked left and right. Murray's lips were pressed tightly together, and the wrinkles on his forehead showed how deeply he was concentrating. Sibley thought that the major was thinking about the coming clash, but he was wrong.

Major Murray was devoutly hoping with all his heart that the deaths waiting for the Chiricahua down in the little meadow over the ridge would not only inflame those off-reservation Apaches who were trying to keep out of trouble as best they could but also force even the reservation Apaches onto the warpath. If that happened, all Arizona would go up in flames. Then everything he had planned and prayed for would fall neatly into place.

# 8

It was midday and hot. Everyone had retired within the *wickiups* until the worst of the heat would pass. Slocum had been watching Kazshe slice his venison. She passed her forearms across her sweating face and stopped.

"Enough!" she said. She looked approvingly at Slocum. "You are strong enough now to make babies." Her broad brown face with its black eyes crinkled in amusement. "There is no Apache girl you like. If you like Dilchay, it must then be so." Dilchay was sitting outside, quietly sewing with deer sinew on the sole of an old Apache boot.

"Dilchay told me what happened when Nachodise came. Try it again tonight. We need babies. Yours will be strong."

The bluntness of the Apaches in dealing with sexual matters was a quality Slocum admired, yet he was unable to accept it as calmly as they did.

Dilchay lifted her eyes from her sewing and looked at him. She was leaning against her *wickiup* in the shade. She had heard Kazshe's remark, and her bold stare made Slocum blush. The two women began to laugh. Their combined amusement was too much for him to bear. He stood up abruptly, and their laughter increased. As he walked out of the *wickiup*, Dilchay leaned forward and grabbed his ankle.

"Tonight we will make a baby!" she called out, not bothering to be discreet.

Slocum liked the idea, but he was used to making the first approach in these matters. These Apache customs took time to adjust to. He pulled his ankle out of her grip and walked toward the chaotic, jumbled maze of giant boulders that the Pima scouts had observed earlier. Reaching them, he climbed the biggest one. Its flat top was the size of two billiard tables placed side by side. He liked that rock. It was hot up there, but he was exposed to the wind that moved across the meadow and up the slope till it spilled over the ridge.

Once there, Slocum sighed and lay flat. He was higher than anyone in the *rancheria*. He had climbed the rock a few times before when he couldn't stand the incessant cheerful babble in the *rancheria*. He let his gaze roam among the big sawteeth of peaks in the far distance. Big snowy galleons of cumulus clouds sailed slowly westward. Once they hit that range, they would be forced to climb. Then they would drop their moisture. The valley below those mountains must be quite a sight, Slocum thought—rich, green, and filled with grass that would come to a man's waist when he rode through it on a horse! It would be a great place for a ranch. He toyed with the idea of pulling one more caper: a big one, preferably in the Northwest, where he wasn't known. After the split, come back here, buy the valley—sixty, seventy thousand might do it. Marry Dilchay, teach her white ways. Take Kazshe in to live with them. He'd send the kids off to an Eastern school. No blizzards to worry about.

He sat up abruptly. He had seen something flash in the distance. He stood for a better view. As soon as he saw the long line of skirmishers, Slocum knew he had seen a rifle barrel.

Those goddamn kids! But there was no time to figure out whose fault it was. He had to let the *rancheria* know immediately. He stood up and cupped his hands around his mouth to yell a warning. There would be no parleying with that silent, murderous line of steadily advancing soldiers. The blue line was only five hundred feet from the *wickiups*. Slocum, who had been a soldier, recognized good planning and scouting. He knew as if he had been there that the Pima scouts had gotten rid of the sentinels.

As he filled his lungs for a warning shout, he felt a tremendous blow on his right thigh. It felt as if a powerful man had suddenly swung a sledgehammer at him with all his might. His leg flew backward. He lost balance and fell into a cleft that separated two boulders. A second later he heard the blast of the Springfield rifle that had shot him.

He fell down the cleft head first, trying to break the fall with his outstretched arms. As Slocum fell, several thoughts flew through his mind. He was sure that he had suffered a very serious wound. Anyway, the sound of the shot must have alerted the camp, though probably it was too late. Most of all, he knew that he was helpless. At the bottom of the cleft there was a small overhang from his boulder. Anyone looking straight down from above would probably not know about that and would assume that no one was down there. He would be invisible.

The skin had been scraped off his palms. They were bleeding from the impact of the rubble-strewn ground. That was all right. They had broken his head-first fall. He looked at his leg. As he suspected, it was broken. But he was lucky; it was not a compound fracture. The bone had stopped the heavy Springfield slug. The inspection took no more than four seconds. Then Slocum turned his attention to the *rancheria*.

Heavy firing had begun. The overhang ran along the bottom of the boulder; the boulder in turn sat on a slight rise. From his vantage point, he could see the *rancheria*, the meadow, and the little creek. Soldiers were running and firing. Little puffs of smoke erupted from their carbines. Whoever had shot him was a marksman and had brought his Springfield. Slocum wanted to meet up with him some day.

No firing was coming from the *rancheria*. He could see the Apaches running. Some had run away from the sound of the shot that had broken his leg, but their course had taken them right into the remaining arc of the skirmish line. Panicking, they ran back. The soldiers shot and bayonetted with a wild frenzy that Slocum did not remember seeing even in hot combat during the Civil War. The men were yelling and cursing. The women fought with knives if they had them. Others fought with whatever had come into their hands in the first few seconds of the attack. Slocum saw sticks of firewood, clay jars, even stones.

Then he saw Kazshe. In her right hand she held the knife she had been using to cut the venison.

Three soldiers surrounded her. She swung her knife upward at the nearest one. He was startled at her sudden expert thrust; he stumbled backward and fell. From a sitting position he fired once, hitting her in the stomach.

Slocum smashed his fist against the boulder. There was absolutely nothing he could do to save her. The situation only allowed him to remember their faces, but he was too far away to do anything else.

Kazshe walked to a tree and sat down. She leaned against it, holding her stomach. She began singing. Slocum knew that it was her death song. The soldiers stared at her.

Major Murray walked up. Slocum recognized him; he wore no hat, and he was fat, with a shaggy brown mustache. "Kill the old bitch and keep moving, you men!" he shouted.

One of the men lifted his carbine. Slocum closed his eyes. When he opened them again, Kazshe lay on her side, absolutely still. Nothing moved in the *rancheria* except the soldiers, who prodded their bayonets at the motionless bodies. Occasionally someone shouted, "This one's still alive!" Then the man would either shoot or bayonet the wounded body. Suddenly Slocum saw Dilchay. She was screaming.

"Bring that squaw here," Murray yelled. "And tie her up, damn you for a bunch of clumsy fools!"

The men lashed her wrists behind her.

"*Donde están los hombres?*" he demanded. "Where are the men?"

She cursed in Apache.

"*Diga me, puta!* Tell me, whore!" All the Chiricahua spoke some Spanish. She spat in his face.

"All right," Murray said heavily. "You men, look

around for anyone who's still alive. Remember what the Sioux did to Custer and his men. Get them all. I want them all dead. Get moving! I'll make this one talk." They walked away.

Suddenly she turned and tried to run. Murray was surprisingly agile and quick for a man of his weight. With one long stride he was in front of her. His foot shot out and swung brutally upward. The pointed toe of his boot caught Dilchay in the shin. She gasped in pain and collapsed on her back. On the top of a nearby *wickiup* some woman had idly tossed a rawhide *reata*. Murray took out a jackknife and cut off two ten-foot lengths. He half carried, half dragged her to the nearby pinyons. He selected two trees with trunks ten feet apart. He tied her ankles to the trees so that her legs were wide apart. Slocum was sick with hopeless rage. Murray took his knife and cut off her skirt. Underneath, the lovely pale brown skin was naked. He could see the black triangle of her pubic hair and the faint pink of her labia. An erection began to bulge outward.

Murray took his pants down, kneeled between her spread thighs, and took out his penis. It was big and hard, and he thrust deeply, with violence. She moaned. She was dry inside. She bit her lips until the blood trickled down her chin.

Murray rammed harder and harder. Sweat slid down his back and turned his blouse black. The dust under Dilchay's naked hips mingled with his sweat and smeared her with a wet, gray coating through which sweat continued to trickle. Finally Murray came with a long drawn-out scream.

He subsided on top of her. Slocum could see her eyes staring up at the blue sky. They showed absolute despair and hatred. Murry stood and pulled up his pants.

"*Le gusta?*" he asked. "Did you like it?" She did not respond.

"Stupid squaw."

He buttoned his fly. Dilchay continued to stare at the sky, even though Slocum knew that the burning sun was not a good thing to look at directly in Arizona.

Still looking at the sky, she said quietly, "*Quiero lavarme.* I want to wash."

"Getting sensible, eh?" he said in English. "All right. You look filthy. No tricks. I might even let you go. You might as well spread the word about what happened here. Might as well be you."

She lowered her eyes and stared at him without understanding.

"*Al agua!*" he ordered. "To the water!" He untied her.

Slocum knew what she was going to do. *Don't do it, Dilchay!* he pleaded silently. I'll get even. Don't do it!

Murray pulled out his revolver. "*No anda!*" he said in his poor Spanish. "Don't run!"

She waded in up to her shoulders. Don't. Slocum willed as hard as he could. She ducked under the surface. But it was no use, none of Slocum's prayers worked. The major was slower to realize what was happening.

When a minute had passed without her surfacing, Murray finally guessed. He yelled for men. Three appeared, panting and exultant.

"There's a squaw down there, find her fast!" he ordered. Then he walked across the *rancheria* to talk to Sibley.

After five minutes they found her and dragged

her onto the bank. She had filled her lungs with water as soon as she ducked under. Their clumsy attempts at resuscitation were a failure. The men stood around her, staring. Her arms were stretched above her head in the same position in which they had dragged her ashore. Her wet blouse was sticking to her body. Some of her shining black hair fell over her left shoulder, covering her left breast. Her lips were slightly parted.

"Not a bad-lookin' little pussy," the corporal said.

The major came back with Sibley. He looked down at her. "Dead?"

The men nodded. "Well," the major said softly. "Damn. Goddamn. All right. Get dressed." Then he added harshly, "Sibley!"

"Sir?"

"Tell the men to take everything they think might be useful to them when they come slinking back. Pile them up and burn them."

Lieutenant Carter, relieved that he was still alive after his first battle, asked, "Shall we burn those, those brush shelters, sir?"

"No," Murray said. "Sibley'll explain why." He left on his tour of inspection.

"We don't burn them because Apaches died here. Whenever an Apache dies, the whole *rancheria* gets burned down. Then they all move elsewhere. The major wants to make it clear when the Apaches come back here that he won't do their work for them. On the other hand," Sibley continued with distaste, "if he was operating against a tribe with permanent houses, like the Zuñis, why, he'd burn their houses right fast, would our major."

He looked down at Dilchay. "Get a detail and bury that poor girl," he said.

"I don't think the major would want that," Car-

SLOCUM AND THE MAD MAJOR 71

ter said. "He told me he wants to make an object lesson—"

"Listen, you squirt, you see that the girl is buried. Tell the men to use bayonets, by God, or I'll run your ass ragged. And if Murray wants to know why you're doing it, you just tell him it was all my idea! Got it?"

"Yes, sir," Carter said sullenly.

Slocum's leg was beginning to hurt. No, he decided, hurt was not the right word. It was an agony such as he had never before experienced. Yet bad as it was, and knowing that he would have to fix it himself and survive, the anguish and rage he felt against Major Murray had assumed gigantic proportions.

Suddenly Murray was back.

"Wasn't that a white man you shot?"

Slocum heard the response, "Yeah. I think so, Major."

"You figure him for one of those white renegades?"

"Yes, sir."

"Well, go up there and find the bastard. If he's still alive, take care of that."

Slocum had been moaning very quietly. Such noises helped to relieve the crashing waves of pain that were driving upward from his smashed femur. The shock period was over; now the pain was really beginning. He clamped his lips tightly shut. He withdrew his head even deeper into the shadow of the overhang. He heard Morrissey clambering up the rubble-strewn slope. Then there was silence. Morrissey was on the boulder itself.

"Well?" Murray called up impatiently.

"I got him," Morrissey said stolidly. "Blood here on the rock, you bet! Blood on the rock goin' down.

He fell. See, he scraped against the rock goin' down. He fell down there."

Slocum was sure that Morrissey was pointing down to where he was lying. Slocum was afraid even to breathe, as if even that minuscule sound might reveal his hiding place. He never underrated dangerous, intelligent opponents. A man who could shoot like Morrissey and who had spent a long time in the frontier army was clearly no fool.

"I don't see no more blood. I bet he took off along the rocks there and under the trees and then over the ridge. Don't see no trail on the rocks. No blood."

"Shit," Murray said. "He's way off now. He made a bandage and ran. Just a flesh wound, probably. But still, he must have noticed something. I lost the girl, but he'll tell them what happened. All for the best, all for the best! Let him go. Sergeant, come on down. Sibley, any casualties?"

"No. A couple men scratched and one bitten by a squaw. That's all."

"When we get back, see to it that they're disinfected. Those little buggers are poisonous." He put his fists on his hips and surveyed the smoking piles of Apache clothing, pots, and food. "A good morning's work, eh, Sibley?"

"Yes, sir," Sibley muttered.

## 9

Slocum watched Murray's troops climb out of the valley. It was still early in the afternoon. His eye told him that it was about one-thirty. One-thirty! Only one hour had passed. In that hour so many lives had ended. The two Apache women with whom his life had been intertwined had died shamefully and in agony, and he had not done anything to prevent it or to help them. He smashed his hand against the rock. That seemed to steady him a bit.

He had to splint his leg and then get out fast. The war party might be back soon. If the Apaches found him, they would kill him, because he was a symbol standing for the white soldiers who had done this, even though no personal guilt might be attached to him. Or Nachodise might think that Slocum had betrayed the band on the principle that blood was thicker than water and had told Murray where to find the Chiricahua. Whatever

## 74 JAKE LOGAN

the reason, if they found him, Slocum knew that he would die.

Slocum crawled down to the *rancheria*. He might be seen by a Pima scout who would have stayed behind to pick off any returning Apaches, but this was a risk he had to take. He had nothing to splint his leg with among the rocks. He was careful not to bang the leg against anything. The biggest problem was not the pain but the strong probability that the jagged edge of bone would break through the skin. If that should happen, he would be finished; there would be no way to prevent gangrene. He had seen enough of that in the war. He could set his own leg. He had seen enough doctors set the legs of cowpunchers who'd had their horses roll over on them. As a matter of fact, Slocum had set legs himself when there was no possibility of getting a doctor or when the nearest one was a drunkard.

He crawled along on his belly. Inch by inch, he snaked his way among the rocks. He suddenly realized that he was very thirsty. It took him an hour and a half to reach the creek, where he drank long and thirstily. Someone must have been bayonetted in the creek farther up. He tasted blood. Nevertheless, he drank. It took another half hour to reach the nearest *wickiup*. Slocum reached up and snapped off a branch. Using it as an extension of his hand, he rested on one elbow and neatly plucked off a *riata* from the roof that the soldiers had missed in their search and destroy mission. He had nothing to cut it with. In fifteen minutes he had chewed it through. He chewed again for another fifteen minutes as fast as he could. He wanted to be out of there before Nachodise returned. His jaws ached, but in half an hour he had

## SLOCUM AND THE MAD MAJOR 75

two manageable lengths of rawhide. He reached up and pulled out three more branches from the *wickiup* walls. Next, he needed a probe to remove the bullet. He crawled carefully, looking for a piece of narrow metal that he could heat in the still smoldering fires.

To his delight, Slocum saw Kazshe's knife in the glowing embers. He fished it out with a stick. The point was still red hot. So much the better; it would cauterize the wound as it probed. He wrapped a length of rawhide around the blade. The wooden hilt and been burned off. He leaned back against the *wickiup* wall, ripped up his pants leg, and exposed the red oozing hole in his thigh. He gritted his teeth and plunged the narrow blade deep into the hole, feeling something move under the tip. He hoped to God it was not his broken femur. Whatever it was moved back and forth under the knife's pressure. It would not come out. If he had a pair of tweezers—but tweezers were not an article commonly found in the *rancherias* of Chiricahua Apaches. He laughed sardonically at the thought; it helped distract him from the pain.

No, the bullet would not come out. Slocum withdrew the blade and looked at it. It was still hot, but his blood had cooled out some of its red-hot color. He would have to act quickly before the blade cooled, thus adding to the chance of infection.

Suddenly Slocum knew what he had to do. Nothing else would serve. He slid the knife in once more. It was a very sharp knife. He knew that; he had sharpened it for Kazshe only yesterday on a piece of natural carborundum he had found. She did not know the special quality of the stone, and when he showed her and gave it to her, she immediately displayed it, proudly proclaiming the intelligence of her adopted son.

Slocum pushed this memory away. He made four quick, deep slices in his thigh. Each cut began at the bullet and ran up through the flesh to the skin. The blood began to gush upward. He hoped that he had not cut any arteries. But there was no help for it; it had to be done. He slid the blade back into the hot coals. He rolled over onto his stomach, reached under to his thigh, gripped the four segmented pieces of flesh, and pulled them as far apart as he could.

Theoretically, the bullet should have fallen out through the wide opening he had created. The agony was as bad as anything he had ever experienced. He permitted himself the luxury of a moan. Nothing fell out. Even gravity was against him. He was rapidly losing strength and was afraid that he might faint. If he did, he might die from loss of blood. Slocum knew that he had only one more chance.

He raised his hips as high as he could and drove them at the stony soil as if he were screwing it. Nothing. Again. Nothing. On the fifth try, the bullet fell out. He lay there a moment, weak, sweating, and exultant. He held his thigh. Sweat drenched his shirt and pants. His hands were wet with blood from the grossly enlarged wound. He rested, taking long sobbing breaths. The blood made the ground soggy under him. He rolled over on his back, still holding on to his thigh. He knew that he had to be extremely careful lest he force a compound fracture through his carelessness and agony. He reached into the fire, took the knife out of the coals and plunged its red-hot length into the four cuts he had made. The blood stopped flowing.

Good. He had successfully cauterized it. He took the four branches, placed them around his thigh, and then wound the rawhide lengths tightly around the wood. When he finished, he had a rigid splint.

Slocum reached up to the walls of the *wickiup* and pulled down a corner post. He inched himself to the next corner and pulled down another one. The posts had been chosen because of their natural Y forks. After Slocum had cut them down to the proper length, he had two serviceable crutches. Now he could move upright.

Feeling somewhat better, Slocum hitched himself as quickly as he could move to the marshy borders of the creek. After several minutes of intense searching, he found what he was looking for—a tiny, three-petaled flower growing out a rosette of five round leaves. The plant hugged the ground and was hard to find. It grew only in damp areas. Kazshe had once shown it to him and said that it was very good for infections. She called it *ikwalquis*.

He picked all he could find, shoved it in a pocket, and then swung back to the *rancheria*. He forced himself to disregard the crumpled, grotesque bodies that lay scattered everywhere. Flies had already settled on the bloody wounds.

The soldiers had smashed the drying racks, but the meat had not been touched. Slocum tied the bottom of his pants legs with twisted grass stems and then filled the legs with as much jerky as he could find. He figured that he had about twenty pounds of the strips. It should last almost three weeks for someone who was not active. He found an unbroken clay pot in a corner of a *wickiup* that had escaped the soldiers. The pot, as Slocum could tell by the design, must have been traded down from the Hopi mesas. He filled it with water, tied a scorched piece of deerskin over it so that it wouldn't spill, and made a rawhide sling, which draped over one shoulder. All the blankets had been burned. That was bad. The nights were very chilly at that altitude. But there was no help for it.

At least he had food, water, medicine, and an effective pair of crutches. He had Kazshe's knife. He could be in worse shape. Now he had to get under the ledge before Nachodise came back. It was a good hiding place. There was no way to trail him across its rock surface. If it rained, he would be reasonably dry. He would be able to keep a good lookout. He could have done a lot worse. He would have to use his belly for a blanket, but he was used to that. It was no great hardship.

It would be hard to stay there. He wanted to get away from the sight of the bodies. But if he moved now, he had no doubt that Nachodise would pick up his trail and follow it as soon as Slocum left the rock surface. Slocum would have to wait till the Chiricahua had come and gone. Then it would be safe for him to find a place where he could lick his wounds, a place where neither Apache nor white soldier would come.

But even that was not so hard. The hardest thing would be to accomplish the task he had set for himself. After he could move, he would find Major Murray and take his life in revenge for Kazshe and Dilchay. He would have to work that part out very carefully. The major was very smart and very tough, even though Slocum was sure that he was insane. He was not the sort of a man to drop his vigilance for a second.

Yet here Slocum was: a broken thigh, no horse, no gun, not a penny in cash, a strong possibility that gangrene might develop. He was also soon to be surrounded by a group of murderous Chiricahuas.

The best thing would be to take care of his leg. The rest would follow.

## 10

Slocum placed the jerky in a pile near his head. The constant wind up there would keep the deerflies with their red-hot stings away. He realized that he hadn't eaten since the evening before. He stuck a piece in his mouth and sliced off a length with Kazshe's knife. The pungent flavor made him salivate heavily. That was good; much saliva was necessary for the plant medicine. He put the blue petals of the *ikwalquis* in his mouth and chewed till it became a soggy mass.

When he had made the splint, he deliberately lashed it to leave a wide gap where he cut into the wound. Now Slocum began pushing the *ikwalquis* into the four gashes. After three chewings, he ran out of saliva. He stripped the deerskin cover from his water jar and took a small mouthful. He remembered Kazshe's warning about too much water:

"The *ikwalquis* god doesn't like water. He lives

beside it and doesn't want any more. He wants something from your body. He has given himself; that is enough. Now you must give him something of yourself."

Slocum had nodded patiently. He had been skeptical of all religious, metaphysical explanations, but now he was not so sure. He had figured that the medicine worked only when it had been combined with an ingredient in the saliva—perhaps an acid, although it didn't really matter. It didn't matter how Kazshe had phrased it. She was right.

He made the poultice and shoved it deep into the wound. He had to sip four times before he made enough *ikwalquis* medicine to do the job properly, the way he had seen Kazshe do it.

The pain was severe. Each time he forced the chewed-up petals into the wound, it felt as if molten lead were sliding into it. When he finally finished, he was dripping with sweat, even though it was cool under the rock overhang. He lay back, panting like a dog. He was going to have a very bad afternoon and a very bad night ahead of him. The only way he could bear it was to think about Major Murray. Thinking about the major would not do much good until he knew a lot more about him: his background, his style of living, his beliefs, and why a man like that would deliberately set out to kill harmless women and children. It made no sense.

The army's job was to patrol the frontier, not to provoke the Chiricahua into fighting, especially such tough men as the Chiricahua, among whom a fourteen-year-old boy, because of his strength and training, could easily handle a mature cavalryman in hand-to-hand combat. Slocum shook his head angrily. It made no sense whatsoever.

There was one good thing about his project: No one knew what Slocum looked like. That was a very good card to hold. He would have to play that hole card carefully as soon as his leg healed. He would have to think about staying alive right now. As soon as the jerky ran out, he would have to become a hunter. A man on crutches armed only with a knife would not make a good hunter.

He managed to sleep, but only fitfully. Once he had a nightmare in which he saw Dilchay coming up out of the creek with her long, black hair dripping. She was staring at him. Slocum struggled to say something, but, tired of waiting for him to talk, she slowly sank back into the water. Once Kazshe came. She stood beside him and said calmly, "My son, avenge me."

He struggled to get out the words: "I will! I will!" But nothing came out of his mouth. She stood looking down at him sadly, and then she smiled. "Ah," she said, "you use *ikwalquis* the way I showed you. That is good." Then she walked away. Slocum cried out, "Kazshe!" She did not stop, nor did she give any indication that she had heard him. Kazshe was the closest thing to a mother Slocum had met in twenty years. Once he woke up during the chilly night and realized that his face was wet with tears. He lay there astonished. He had not cried since he had come home to Mississippi at the end of the war and found out that his mother had died. He finally fell asleep. He woke up suddenly to the sound of voices.

The Chiricahau were returning. They had not realized what had happened till they came close; after all, the *wickiups* were still standing. He heard Nachodise angrily denouncing the absent sentinels. He was saying what he would do to them when he saw them. That meant that he still did not realize what had happened.

Then one man saw the footprints left behind by the skirmish line as they had advanced. He called out softly in an urgent tone. All the men went prone immediately. Nachodise gave an order. Eskiminzin, Kazshe's nephew, moved forward. His duty was to draw fire and expose the ambush positions of the cavalry.

"Tracks are old," he called out. He was the first one to see the bodies.

The others ran up at his cries. Slocum turned his head away. He did not want to see their grief.

"Where is the white man's body?" Nachodise demanded. "Find it!" When the men reported that it was not to be found, Nachodise said, heavily, "I told you. He led the soldiers here. I will look for him. Now bring all the bodies here."

The bodies were placed in one *wickiup*. The men tore apart the other *wickiups* and piled the dried brushwood above the mound of corpses. Nachodise took out a match and struck it. Slocum was so close that he could smell the sharp whiff of sulphur. When the funeral pyre was blazing strongly, the Apaches took out their warpaint. Nomadic people do not keep cemeteries; there is no strong respect for the dead.

Nachodise took a piece of broken mirror from his pouch. With two broad fingers he traced a broad streak of paint across his face, from the outside corner of each eye to the hard-bitten ends of his mouth. When he was finished, he replaced the paint and the mirror. He stood up. "Now we can go," he said harshly.

God help any whites they meet, Slocum thought. No prisoners would be taken. Of that he was absolutely sure.

## 11

Slocum decided to spend the night under the overhang, just to play it safe. It was a terrible night; the agony was almost unbearable. He shivered most of the night; sleep was impossible. In the morning, as soon as there was enough light, he looked at his leg. It was not swollen and puffy as he had feared. On the contrary, the skin around the wound looked pink and healthy. Now that he thought about it, he was almost sure that the pain had lessened a bit compared to what he had been feeling during the night.

During the night he had clasped himself with both arms and gone into the fetal position to try to keep some body heat from escaping. Somehow he would have to find shelter while his leg healed. Looking for a white habitation was out of the question. Since his bank robbery had failed, there must have been treason; if there was treason, there had to be a reward out with his description. Because of his reputation, a handsome reward was no doubt being offered. Slocum did not want to place temptation in anyone's path.

No, Slocum thought, he would have to live alone, supply all his own wants, and avoid all white contact while his leg healed. Food, lodging, warmth, safety. He had food for a while. Not moving around would conserve energy. Thank God, he would not need much food. Water would not be a problem in the high mountains. Clouds would discharge their water; there would be creeks and even small lakes. Warmth could be supplied by fire, but fire and smoke would attract roving bands of Apaches or soldiers. There would be no fires. He did not want to have to deal with either group until he was ready.

He looked out from the overhang. Not even a wisp of smoke from the *wickiups*. No sign of life. A few buzzards lazily circled overhead, and the wind was blowing. That was all. The Apaches had returned to the earth whence they had sprung. It was time to go.

High up on the mountains to the west would be the best course. There he would be away from the traveled roads and trails and away also from the white-traveled military roads. High up, the higher the better. That way safety lay.

He struggled to his feet and stuck the knife in his belt without a scabbard. He would have to make one soon or lose his only weapon and tool. The jerky strips went into his pants legs. Regretfully he left the clay jar behind. It was convenient but not necessary. He made his way up the narrow gap between the two huge boulders down which he had slid—was it only the day before yesterday?

—by bracing his shoulders and one knee against the opposite rock. He could not have done it by tying his crutches to his belt; the weight would have been too much. He had simply dropped them over the ledge just beyond the overhang. Somehow he would get to them.

It took Slocum an hour of struggle to reach the top of the boulder. He rested, panting, for half an hour. Jerky was all right to survive on, but it certainly would not do for serious bursts of physical energy. For that he would need meat with plenty of fat—a bear, for instance. By now the bears that had hibernated in the mountains had put back most of the fat they had lived on during the winter in their caves. A nice bit of bear steak, well-larded with bear fat—Slocum began to salivate as he thought about it. Then he laughed. There was no way he was going to handle a grizzly with a knife. There were some Apaches who had done that and were therefore entitled to wear the claws in the form of a necklace. But in all his years in the West, Slocum had only seen one man with a bear-claw necklace. And that man had had terrible scars.

Slocum reached the bottom of the rocks and picked up the crutches. His progress was painfully slow. It was a valley floor, all right, but when he began limping across it, he became aware of the stones, clumps of *sacaton* grass, and prairie dog holes—the sorts of things that a man on horseback never notices, and that a well man on foot disregards as extremely minor. A few times a crutch went deep into a prairie dog tunnel, just below the surface. Slocum fell each time. It hurt like a son of a bitch, but, he suddenly realized with a feeling of pleasure, it didn't hurt as much as it had yesterday. It had to be Kazshe's medicine that was doing it, and it must also have some sort of a narcotic effect. He felt depressed. He had been trying hard not to think about the women, and he had almost succeeded for a while. He wrenched his mind away from the two women and locked it into the task of movement.

The only way to prevent falling was to test the ground first with a probe of one crutch while he balanced himself on his good leg. It was a painfully slow way to move, but at least he did not fall any more. And if he were to suffer a bad fall, he might undo all the healing Kazshe's *ikwalquis* had accomplished.

Once the crutch end went into a prairie dog hole, and he felt a sudden thud at the end. When he pulled it out, a four-foot rattler was clinging to it. The fangs had been driven so deeply into the soft wood that the snake couldn't pull them out. Slocum whirled the crutch around his head. The fangs snapped off, and the rattler sailed away, coiling and twisting till it landed with a thump thirty feet away.

By late afternoon Slocum had moved four miles. Unfortunately, he had left a trail anyone could follow. He stopped and ate four strips of jerky, halfway up the slope of the big mountain that Kazshe had called Dzil Ligai. She had said that it was a sacred mountain. Slocum hoped that meant that Apaches would not visit there. Apaches believed in all kinds of spirits. He suddenly remembered that Kazshe had told him that Dzil Ligai was the home of the wind and the mountain spirits. He did not remember whether mountain spirits were good or bad. If they were bad, that was good. The superstitious Apaches would avoid the mountain. But if they were good spirits, he might have unpleasant visitors. But he needed a big mountain where he could hide and find water, and the other peaks looked too small. Dzil Ligai it had to be.

He kept climbing slowly and painfully. He did not look back once. That part of his life was over. After he had avenged Kazshe and Dilchay, he might come back, but not until then.

He was very thirsty. A tiny, ice-cold trickle appeared across his route. He bellied down slowly and carefully. It bubbled along under some big pines. He drank his fill and then wiped his mouth and looked around. It would be dark soon and he would have to find a place to sleep. He could cut off enough soft pine tips to make a sort of a mattress, but there was no way he could get warm. He dared not risk making a fire in the open. He had no matches, but long ago an Ogalala had shown him how to make a fire drill. There was enough dry powdered wood in the fallen pines so that the friction of the swiftly spinning drill would set it alight.

No fires, not until he found a cave. A cave would be a safe place to make a fire. He would like a cave very much; he set himself the task of looking for one. Caves were not that easy to find; if there was a small opening, trees and shrubs would frequently mask it.

But for once luck was with him. He found a cave within ten minutes, set within the rock face to his left. The setting sun had sent its horizontal rays into it, or he would not have noticed it, since the opening was screened by several pine trunks. Slocum decided that the mountain spirits of the Apaches were friendly spirits. He had filled one pocket with the dried, powdered wood he had found in the fallen pines. A mile away from the cave he had picked up an eighteen-inch length of oak. It was the correct length for a drill and was as thick around as his thumb. A chunk of soft pine wood with a flat top and bottom would be perfect for a base for the fire drill.

"You damn fool," he said aloud. "What do you think this is, a lumberyard?" Yet he found it quickly. It was under a pine tree that had been struck by lightning long ago. It had exploded, and one piece had been shaped exactly to his specifications. Slocum felt a shiver of awe. No wonder the Apaches said that Dzil Ligai was a sacred mountain. He began to feel kindly toward it. He limped toward the cave opening. He took out his knife and, holding it in his mouth, he slowly moved into the cave. He had smelled bear.

But it was old bear smell. Probably the sow had hibernated here, given birth to a couple of cubs, and then gone off with them in the spring to feast on prairie dogs, fish, and blackberries.

He tossed in a few stones he had picked up outside. No response. He pulled out another stone, somewhat bigger than the first one, balanced himself carefully, and threw it as hard as he could. It went in a long way before it clattered down. Silence. Good! It was a big cave, curved a bit, and he could make a fire there without being noticed. Maybe someone could spot it if he was standing at exactly the same spot, directly opposite Dzil Ligai, but a man had to take chances sometimes.

Limping here and there, he picked up an armful of dead wood from under the pines. Unfortunately, pine would burn too quickly. But a few trips enabled him to pile up enough wood to last the night.

Satisfied, Slocum found a small curved branch. This would form the bow of the drill. He tied a piece of the invaluable rawhide to each end. He limped inside the cave and sat down with a grunt of relief. He took the piece of flat pine that Dzil Ligai had given him and gouged out a hole in the center with his knife. Into the hole he placed a few pinches of the powdered wood. He wound the string of the rawhide once around the oak stick, and then he put the flat of his calloused left palm atop the oak drill. He made sure that the head of the drill was on the edge of the palm, away from his puncture wound.

He set the bottom of the oak into the loose wood powder and sawed the drill back and forth. It spun amazingly fast. In fifteen seconds a trickle of smoke came from the powder. In thirty seconds a tiny red spark was born.

Slocum bent forward and blew gently. The added oxygen fed the spark, and it grew bigger. When it was doing nicely, he carefully spilled it onto a tiny latticework of dried twigs he had prepared. After the twigs had caught fire, he carefully added larger twigs. When they were burning, he added small branches. In five minutes he had a warm fire going.

Satisfied, he limped outside to see whether the fire could be noticed. He moved to one side and then the other. He was invisible. Then he limped painfully down the slope. Invisible! Slocum felt exultant. As he turned to climb up again, his crutch hit a small pile of stones and then another pile.

He remembered what Kazshe had told him about Dzil Ligai. Apaches, she had said, came long distances and piled stones into little altars, to signify that it was a holy place.

"Well," Slocum said aloud. "Goddamnit to hell."

He very well might have visitors during his convalescence.

## 94  JAKE LOGAN

\* \* \*

His first visitors showed up early the next morning.

He had slept well for two reasons: the warmth of the fire and the lessening pain in his leg. What woke him was a light scuffling sound and some low growls. He opened his eyes and grabbed the knife. If there was any fighting, he would have to do it sitting up. There was no way he could do anything on crutches.

Two small furry shapes were outlined at the cave entrance. Their light-brown fur made it clear that they were grizzlies. They were wrestling and snarling like puppies. Slocum relaxed for a moment before it struck him that cubs so young must have a mother close at hand. And a sow grizzly with young cubs was absolutely predictable. She would charge immediately.

His only chance was to urge the cubs to go elsewhere, but he had to do it in such a way that they would go peacefully and not howl in fear or anger. Any such tone in their voices would be the end. At any rate, he would have to get out of the cave fast. If she came back into her winter home— which, no doubt, she knew inside out—she would pin him down with a rush and rip him apart with her five-inch claws, curved and sharp as scimitars.

Out in the open he would have a chance—not much of one, but certainly better than anything he would have inside the cave. He might be able to climb a tree, even with his leg in splints. Outside was his only hope. Slocum sat erect and painfully struggled to an upright position. He put the knife in his teeth. He could not risk losing it. The cubs still had not noticed him. They were locked in a ball of brown fur, digging each other in the belly with their baby claws and biting each other's necks. Slocum didn't want to scare them. The cubs would go off howling to their mother. He began humming as he slowly approached. The sound was low and pleasant. Horses and dogs had been soothed by it. It would let them know that he was coming and prevent any panicky, startled cries. They were so busy growling and fighting their mock battle that they did not see or hear him, even though he was only a few feet away.

When Slocum tried to swing by on his crutches, they suddenly burst out into shrill, terrified bawling. They tumbled out of the mouth of the cave.

*That's it!* thought Slocum. He swung as fast as he could on his crutches toward the nearest tree. The lowest branch was seven feet up. He was almost at the tree when he heard a deep, menacing rumble that made his blood run cold. Sure enough, they had come back with their mother. She was moving fast toward him.

There was no way he could outrun a grizzly. Even in perfect shape, he could not have done it. On a straight away, a grizzly could outrun a racehorse in the first hundred yards. In underbrush, where a man would stumble and clamber, a grizzly could crash straight through brush like a locomotive.

He reached the tree. She was fifty feet away and coming like a rocket, moving up the rocky slope like a concentrated massive brown flood. In the silence he could hear her claws clicking against the rock surface. With a sudden burst of speed he reached the tree, but he knew that in his condition he would never make it to the first branch. He spun around, dropped the crutches, and leaned back against the tree trunk in one swift, decisive movement. He took the knife from his teeth and held it low, point upward. The sow, only six feet away now, stood upright. Slocum guessed her height at eight feet. She was outlined by the sun. The ends of her hair shone silver. She took two steps forward. Her small eyes seemed red. Her jaws were wide open. The canine teeth were five inches long.

Slocum leaned toward her suddenly. She did not expect that movement and recoiled a bit. When he leaned back against the tree for support, she waddled angrily toward him and swung both her massive forearms in a swift embracing motion. She was so furious at this strange-smelling threat to her cubs that her depth judgment was impaired. Her two sets of claws drove deeply into the soft pine, and at the same time her chest pressed tightly against Slocum's face. The acrid, rank smell of her fur filled his nose. He slid down a bit, put his left hand behind him against the trunk to steady himself, and with all his strength drove the knife into her lower belly. Then he ripped upward and pulled out the knife.

Her gray, slick guts tumbled out over Slocum's moccasins. But by then he had rammed the knife into her throat up to the hilt and then jerked it savagely sideward. From the sudden jet spray of blood against his face, he knew that he had severed her jugular. She sagged. Her great weight pressed him tightly against the rough trunk. She was held upright by her claws, which were still dug into the tree. She let out a bubbling sound and died.

The stink of her fur filled Slocum's nostrils. He turned his head to be able to breathe, astonished that he was still alive. He pressed hard at her with his head and shoulders. Her claws pulled free, and she fell backward with a heavy thump.

Slocum wiped the blood from his face and chest and took a deep breath. It took a few seconds for him to realize that he had killed a grizzly with a knife. "My God," he whispered aloud. Then he gave the rebel yell.

The noise brought the cubs from the cave, where they had fled for safety as soon as their mother gave the danger growl. They had been born in the cave, and to them it represented security. They ran in the ungainly fashion of young cubs to the prostrate form of their mother. They growled in a worried manner when she did not respond to their nuzzling. Slocum watched them. He faced a problem. He would have liked to let them go, even though their chances of survival in an area where mountain lions prowled and wolves ran in packs would be very small. But if the boar was in the area, the cubs might lead him to the cave.

"And one thing for sure," Slocum said aloud, "I'm never going to kill two grizzlies in a row with a knife."

With regret he killed the cubs.

By late afternoon he had skinned them all. The meat was well marbled, with ivory streaks of fat running through it. They had eaten well since coming out of hibernation. He cut several steaks. In this high, windy place with few flies, they would keep several days. The rest he cut up in strips for jerky and hung them from the dried branches of a pine a great windstorm had blown down long ago. The hot, dry wind would dry them in a couple of days. He broke open her skull with a stone and removed the brains. After he had removed every single particle of meat, fat, and gristle from the inside of her skin, he worked the brains into the skin with a long sliver of stone he had found in the cave. The brains would keep the fur soft and supple when it dried out.

When Slocum went down to the small pond he had found two hundred feet to the left of the cave for a drink, he noticed a small clay deposit. He drank and went back pleased. He was getting tired of making a trip every time he wanted a drink. He hobbled back to the cave, took the skin of one of the cubs, swung back again, and filled the skin with clay. He packed it back. He hobbled out again and gathered enough wood to last the night.

Slocum did not mind any of this. Getting the wood was better medicine for him than thinking about what to do to Murray. And working on the clay would give his hands something to do while he sat by the fire and broiled that first bear steak. When the bearskin tanned out nice and soft, he wouldn't have to gather any more of that damned firewood to keep warm. The fur would become both mattress and blanket.

He shaped the clay into several supple cylinders. Then, working the way he had seen the women making clay jars up in San Ildefonso Pueblo, he made three jars. He started with a small coil of clay for the base; on top he placed a slightly larger coil. Thus he built up a pot. When it was done, he put it close to the fire and looked at it with enormous satisfaction. He had never before realized that the simplest conveniences, which he had always taken for granted, represented long hard work for Indians.

Later, filled with a juicy bear steak, he pushed the three pots closer to the fire for more baking: one for water, one for rendered fat to baste other meats if they were too lean, and one for various grains or fruits he might come across. He decided that he hadn't done badly at all that day for a man with a broken leg. He felt more proud of himself than he had in many years. He had killed a grizzly with a knife!

"By God, John Slocum," he said aloud, "you've earned yourself a bear-claw necklace!"

He had saved the claws. He took Kazshe's knife and began slowly drilling a hole in the first claw. When he had finished the first hole, he lay back for a second to rest. But he was so tired, he fell asleep immediately.

## 12

Three weeks later Slocum threw away the crutches. The bone had knitted perfectly. He had a huge scar in the shape of a plus sign on the front of his thigh, left over from the four deep cuts. There was little pain, and that only when he put too much weight on the wounded leg when walking quickly. That would go away in time. He was amazed at how quickly the leg had healed. He gave the credit to Kazshe's *ikwalquis*. Perhaps there was something in it that was good for bone calcium. And the rich diet of bear meat—now all gone—and berries and wild lemons and an occasional fish from the pond all helped make him heal quickly.

He had also spent plenty of time thinking about how he would approach Murray at Fort Kearney. He would have to do it in such a way that no one would suspect that he was the white renegade Morrissey had shot. No one must suspect that he was also wanted for bank robbery. How to do it? The answer came suddenly out of the blue while he was taking a bath in the pond.

He had scrubbed himself with soap before he went in. He was justly proud of that soap. He had mixed bear fat with wood ashes from the fire. Then he had set it in one of his pots near the fire, and the result the next morning was a viscous scum that was a crude and harsh yet effective soap.

After he had soaped himself, Slocum swam back and forth in the cool water, exercising his leg. He was not worried about spoiling the drinking water. A constant flow kept emptying and refilling the pond. When he was tired, he sat on the shore and rested. When the pond had returned to its mirror surface, his reflection stared back at him. His beard was over two inches long; his hair was almost touching his shoulders. He wore the bear-claw necklace. His pants and shirt had long ago shredded away. He had trapped deer in a deadfall and tanned their skins. Using deer sinew and cutting a pattern with his knife, he had made buckskin pants and a buckskin shirt. When he put on his clothes, he stared at the strange figure with its necklace and long hair.

"Why," he said thoughtfully. "I'm a mountain man."

Now Slocum knew how he would get to Fort Kearney. He would come as a mountain man with furs to sell.

As soon as Slocum had made that decision, he immediately began to hunt for furs. He trapped lynx and cougar in deadfalls. Since the mountain was sacred, it was forbidden to hunt there. All the wild things moved with confidence; they had no fear of his scent.

Two months later he was ready. He bundled his furs into a huge pack that weighed close to 175 pounds. He made a tump line and then strapped the furs to his back. He began to walk toward Major Murray.

## 13

Nachodise had smeared wet clay all over his naked body and worked it into his hair. An hour before sunrise, he arrived outside Fort Kearney. He smeared the head and shaft of his lance with more of the stuff. The lance head had a slight curve to it; it had been made from the sword of a Spanish soldier who had wandered away from De Armijo's expedition to New Mexico in 1567 and died of thirst in the *Jornada del Muerte*. Three hundred years later a Lipan Apache had found the sword clutched in the bones of the man's right hand and he had made a lance out of it. It had been traded to a Mescalero Apache, who had traded it to Nachodise.

By sunrise Nachodise was stretched flat in the chaparral. He could easily see into Fort Kearney. Nachodise was interested in the fort. From there, the soldiers had come who had wiped out his *rancheria*. One month ago a careless, drunken soldier had wandered up the road singing "Green Grow the Rushes, O" and died instantly, impaled on Nachodise's lance. As a result the guard had been doubled. Nachodise knew that they were going to do just that, and for that month he was nowhere near the fort. He went raiding into Mexico and had a good time killing Mexicans. Now that a month was over, they were going to relax their vigilance, and Nachodise was back. He knew how to wait. He had a good view of the fort, and he looked at it carefully.

He could see the guardhouse. He knew that that was where they put the bad soldiers, the ones who had run away. This Nachodise could not understand. If an Apache on the war trail decided that his luck was bad, he simply went home with no hard feelings. In the middle was the parade ground, where they kept practicing with the horses, charging back and forth and dismounting, and then getting on again and getting off as fast as they could. On one side was the enlisted men's barracks. On the other side of the parade ground were the officers' quarters and some nice houses where the married officers lived. On one end of the parade ground was the post trader's store; on the other end were the stables. Up a hill from the stables was the firing range. It was too risky to roam around the fort at night; everyone was armed.

Half an hour after sunrise, the sun had baked the wet clay till it was the same color as the soil. A man could step on Nachodise before realizing that he was there. A beaded black and orange Gila monster paused for a second in the shade cast by Nachodise's body. Its tongue flicked out a few times, trying to identify the strange scent. It gave up and waddled on.

Nachodise had observed something curious about one of the men in the fort. During his days of watching and waiting, the Apache had seen that one of the officers went everywhere surrounded by a bodyguard. Nachodise was too far away to recognize the man as Major Murray, and the Apache's binoculars had been lost on his last raid. There were always six men and a sergeant. They were big men on good horses, and they were well armed. He had seem them at the firing range. They were all marksmen. He was consumed with envy at the number of cartridges they fired off at target practice. He did not want to get near them. They were too good with the carbines and Colts they always carried. At night four of them were always on duty around the house where the officer lived with his woman. She had long red hair. Nachodise thought that he would like to rape her just to make the officer mad. He waited patiently.

Nachodise yawned. He suddenly grew alert. A weird shape loomed down the road. It veered toward the fort, cutting across the valley floor to save time. Its route would take it close by. Nachodise grunted in satisfaction. He slowly drew up his legs for a spring. He was in a good mood. Yesterday afternoon, outside a ranch house near the Mowry Mine, a little girl had come into the house and told her mother that there was an Indian behind the hen coop. "Why, that can't be," her mother had said, and stepped outside. Nachodise's lance went through her from side to side. He took the girl with him. She cried too much and made too much noise, and so he killed her. This morning he would add another white to the balance scale.

As soon as Slocum got within a hundred feet, Nachodise saw that the weird shape was caused by a huge bundle of furs on the man's back. He noticed that the outside wrapping was that of an enormous grizzly and that the man's only weapon was a knife in a deerskin scabbard. The man was so tanned that at this distance he could not be distinguished from an Indian.

But his beard gave him away. The man's clothes were made of buckskin, which he had never seen on a white man, but what riveted the Apache's attention was the bear-claw necklace. The claws were the biggest Nachodise had ever seen. He looked at them in awe. This white man had killed the grizzly himself, and with that little knife! He must have strong medicine. He deserved to live. Moreover, perhaps his medicine would be too strong for Nachodise.

Nachodise remained still, as Slocum passed within eight feet of him. Nachodise decided that no more luck would come his way that day. He slid back through the chaparral, entered a grove of cottonwoods that grew from the meandering river that looped through the valley and assured drinking water to Fort Kearney. He washed off the dry cracked clay and trotted away. There would be other lucky days.

## 14

The post trader was an ex-chemist named Johansen. His doctor in Massachusetts had advised a dry climate for his asthma. Mrs. Johansen would not leave Boston and he had divorced her and opened the store, since there was no demand for a chemist in Arizona. On its shelves were cigars, socks, pipes, underwear, straight razors, and canned goods, especially peaches. Soldiers were fond of canned peaches. There were knives, sardine cans, crackers in a barrel, pickles in a barrel, and similar attractions. Sibley liked Johansen and liked to talk to him when his duties were over for the day. They would sit quietly and play chess.

Behind the trading post was a crude shed where Johansen amused himself with chemical experiments. An occasional explosion enlivened the area and set the horses in the stable plunging and snorting. They had been trained to stand still for carbine and revolver fire, but the occasional dull *boom* from Johansen's shed was too much for them.

Johansen bought the furs immediately. He paid $260 for the lot, which was a very fair price. He especially admired the grizzly skin.

Slocum had said nothing when he brought the furs into the store. He dropped the bale on the floor, cut it open, pointed, and waited. When Johansen made his offer, Slocum nodded. Johansen paid in eight double eagles and five silver dollars.

"You don't have any pockets to put the money in. How about buying a pair of pants?"

Slocum nodded. "Shirt, too," he said. Johansen laid a blue flannel shirt on the counter.

"Boots?"

"Boots."

"Belt?"

"Belt."

"Belt, by God!" Johansen shouted. "Let's get into the spirit of this!"

Slocum bought a complete outfit. He handed back two double eagles and got five more silver dollars in change. He nodded, smiling.

"You don't talk much."

"Nope."

"Mountain man?"

"Guess you can say that."

"Been alone up there?"

"Up where?"

"Dzil Ligai."

"Yep."

"Indians say Dzil Ligai was fastened to the earth with a stone knife."

Slocum's eyes widened in interest. He had a feeling that he would like Johansen.

"Want a snort? Not allowed on the post, but you

look like a man who knows how to keep a secret." He walked to the front door, looked around, came back, and unlocked a cabinet in the back storeroom. He pulled out Wild Turkey, filled two water glasses with the bourbon, handed one to Slocum, held up his glass and said, "Here's death and damnation to the major!" Then he drank.

Slocum drank his slowly and with pleasure. It was good to find an enemy of the major's so soon.

"Don't you like him?"

"My boy, the major fools a lot of people. The troops think he loves them. He loves them the way a man loves a slave who works hard to bring in the cotton. He's as cold-blooded as a rattler with a chill. You hang around here, and you'll see what I'm talking about. A mystery to me, especially with that wife of his. She's a red-headed woman, and let me tell you, son, a red-headed woman in a green dress is the prettiest thing in the world. And she's got a green dress. Wore it at the officer's dance. It's cut real low. Some of the men peeked in the windows at her. You could see some of them wouldn't mind getting themselves a piece of it, even if it cost them a strangulation jig.

"Bet you haven't had a hot bath in months. Why don't you go on over to the post barber and get him to trim those whiskers of yours. After you do that, you can get a bath there. Then come on back here and put on your clean clothes. What say?"

Slocum nodded. His role as a mountain man had worked. He liked Johansen. Maybe he could use Johansen in a way that would enable him to stick around Fort Kearney.

"We'll get rid of that shrubbery, what say?" the barber suggested cheerfully.

And get rid of a damn good disguise? Slocum thought. "Just a little, trim the beard," Slocum said. "An inch, maybe, off the hair."

"That ain't the style," the barber said disapprovingly.

"It's my style," Slocum replied.

There was ice in his voice, and the barber sensed it immediately. He fell silent. Slocum's "Man Wanted" poster showed him clean-shaven and with closely cropped hair. It had been taken in the Wyoming territorial prison two years before. Slocum had taken off several pounds since then. His face was much leaner and harder now. He had passed a winter in Montana just before the picture was taken; therefore, it showed him as pale. Now, with his tan, long hair, less weight, and a beard, he bore no resemblance at all to the picture—except in the eyes, which were still hard and unwavering.

"That's some necklace you got there," said the barber as he snipped away. "Buy it off an Injun?" Without pausing for a response, he said, "Give you five bucks for it."

Slocum turned his head and just looked at him. Most men who had seen the icy calm of those eyes had regretted it.

"Just askin', stranger, just askin'. No need to take on like that when a fellow's tryin' to help. Bein' friendly, is all."

Slocum lost interest in what the barber was saying. The man sighed softly in relief. This was the first mountain man he had ever seen, and he fervently hoped that it would be the last.

"All right, stranger, finished!"

"How much?"

"For bath and soap and towel and hair trim and a beard trim—how does three bucks strike you?"

## SLOCUM AND THE MAD MAJOR   113

"As highway robbery," Slocum said, and smiled at the thought that a real highway robber such as himself had used such a phrase.

"Said it by way of makin' a little joke. Price is two bucks."

Slocum dropped two cartwheels into the barber's hand and left. On the way back to Johansen's, he suddenly stiffened as he saw Major Murray trotting across the parade ground on a superb black mare. Slocum slowed down to absorb all the information he could. Murray rode well. Like Slocum he had been a cavalryman all through the Civil War. He had put on about eight pounds since Slocum had last seen him. His face wore a self-assured, confident look, the look of a powerful man for whom things were going very well. Slocum had seen that look on the emperors on old Roman coins.

Behind Murray's horse rode six troopers. Slocum did not yet know that they were Murray's permanent bodyguard. Unlike most troops Slocum had seen on the frontier, they were very well turned out. Yellow stripes ran down their neatly pressed blue trousers. All of them wore Colts, a weapon usually reserved for officers. None wore sabers. Their horses were in top condition. As Murray reined in to watch a platoon under Lieutenant Carter practice riding in file and rank, the horses of the bodyguard seemed to dance as they worked off their excess energy.

The riders handled them well. They were continually turning in their saddles and watching everything and every direction from which a shot might come. Even Slocum received some sharp glances. They looked over the roof of the enlisted men's barracks and the empty angle between Johansen's store and the nearby laundry. Then they looked Slocum over once more. The sergeant commanding the bodyguard said a quiet word to one of the men. The man went immediately across the parade ground to Slocum.

Reining on, he said casually, "Mornin'."

"Mornin'."

"Stranger here, ain't you?"

"Yep."

"Major wants to know what your business is."

"Trapper."

"You the fellow sold the furs to Johansen?"

"Yep."

"Not meanin' to look curious, hope you ain't offended, but the major wants to know your plans."

Slocum was not used to answering questions like those. It was not the custom of the frontier to probe that way. The soldier was a hard, patient man. He waited, his left hand on the pommel, the other hand on top of the first.

"Nice horse," Slocum observed.

"You ain't answered my question, mister. And you better answer, because this is army property."

That was logical, Slocum thought. It deserved a decent response. "My plans are to find a lost gold mine and take a million dollars out of it. But in answer to your question, I suppose I'll be movin' on soon as I can buy a horse."

"I can take that back to the major. No hard feelin's, mister. I'm much obliged."

He turned and rode back to Major Murray and reported. The major gave Slocum a casual glance and lost interest. There was no way Slocum could kill the major and have the slightest chance of making good his escape. He strolled slowly back to the store, rapidly thinking up and discarding ideas.

None of them would work. Murray would be a very hard nut to crack. It would take lots of time to figure out how to crack him. But he wouldn't be able to stay at the fort; that was clear. Johansen smiled as he walked in.

"You look better," he said. "Listen, where's your rifle?"

"Didn't have any."

"Christ! How come?"

"Apaches jumped me. Took everythin'. I got away."

"Christ again. You spent all that time up there *without* a rifle?"

"Yep."

"Holy jumping mackerel! Sit on that chair and have some sardines and crackers while I digest that information. And you killed that grizzly with that little knife?"

Slocum nodded, and they ate in friendly silence.

"What's your next move?"

Slocum shrugged as two soldiers walked in.

The bigger soldier said, "Give me a couple cans of peaches." He was a tall, broad-shouldered man in his middle thirties. "Got a powerful headache."

Johansen did not move.

The soldier repeated his request, and Johansen said quietly, "As soon as you pay your bill."

"Next payday! Now hurry up and get me them cans afore I get mad."

Johansen reached under the counter and came up with an account book. "Let's see," he said pleasantly. "K, L, M. Ah, here we are. Morrissey, John. Corporal Morrissey—"

"It's back to private."

"It's hard to keep track of your promotions and

demotions, Morrissey. Here we are. You owe me $19.74."

"Said I'll pay you next payday, didn't I?"

"Yes, you told me that. You also told me that the last three paydays."

"A man's got to have a couple drinks now and then and have a little fun with the laundresses. You hold that against me, Johansen?"

"No. And a man's got to be paid."

His friend suddenly asked, "Who's the half-breed with the necklace?"

His words were meant to be taken as an insult, as Slocum well knew.

"He is a friend of mine," Johansen said stiffly.

Morrissey paid no attention. "You one of them renegades? Or are you a half-breed? You got some white blood in you with that beard, that's sure, but it sure smells like piss to me. Give you a buck for the necklace. Buy a handkerchief for your squaw. She'll be glad to hump for that."

He reached out and flicked one of the claws with a dirty fingernail.

"Don't," Slocum said gently.

"Don't!" Morrissey mocked him.

He placed a hand on Slocum's chest and shoved. But Slocum's friend, the Chinese laundryman, had taught him how to deal with that kind of aggression. Slocum spun on one heel, sliding his chest away from Morrissey's palm. His right hand came up and grabbed the corporal's sleeve at the elbow, and an encouraging shove forced Morrissey into a sudden impromptu run. A fraction of a second later, Slocum stuck his foot out, and Morrissey fell flat with a crash that shook the whole store. His friend took a swing at Slocum. Slocum ducked, pivoted, and rammed his right elbow backward into the man's belly. The man let out an agonized grunt and sank to his knees. It all happened within two seconds. When the third second began, Slocum was sitting down again and decorously eating a sardine.

"Well, I'm double-dog damned!" Johansen said.

Morrissey and his friend got up slowly and painfully. They took a long hard look at Slocum.

"Gentlemen," Johansen said, "I tell you one thing. You grab a pickle, and you never know which way it'll squirt."

The two men walked away silently.

Johansen turned to Slocum. "Mind telling me your name?"

"Brian Walker," Slocum said promptly. He always had an authentic-sounding name ready. Names like Joe Smith or Art Jones never had that convincing ring.

"If you're thinking of hanging around here while you build up a stake, I can use a helper."

Slocum put down his can. It looked like the perfect solution for his problem.

"No long-term promises. Stay as long as you feel like it. I need someone around here to keep order and help me out. I'm awful busy working on my chemical experiments in the back, something the army would like very much, and I hate to run into the store every time someone wants a chew of tobacco. It's not good to have stuff stay too long in the test tubes. I'll pay decently, and you can sleep in the back. And I need to dig out a cellar in the back and work in it. Less chance of bad damage if there's an explosion. What say?"

"You got a deal."

## 15

Slocum threw up another shovelful of dirt and paused. He was stripped to the waist.

"What kind of experiments you doin'?" he asked. He took a long swig of cool water from the clay olla that swung, suspended by a rawhide thong, from a nail driven into the back of the trading post.

Johansen was sitting in the storeroom by a window overlooking the back yard. "Like everyone else," he said, putting down a three-week-old Washington newspaper, "I want to make a lot of money from my government. And the way for someone with my chemical education to do that is to make a kind of explosive those idiots can't resist. And what they need is a good, cheap smokeless powder."

"You bet," Slocum said, impressed. With black powder it was very easy to locate an enemy sniper. All a man had to do during the war was direct fire at the white puffs. That was why snipers had a short life expectancy. An explosive charge in a cartridge that wouldn't leave that telltale trace behind it would have immense appeal.

"Not to mention other countries," Johansen added. "Of course, I would never sell my secret to a potential enemy of the United States. I would never, *never*, sell it to Switzerland or Iceland." He lit his pipe. "So that's what I'm doing. But without a Bunsen burner, it's very hard to control my experiments. Using a coke fire for a steady heat is the best I can do, but it's not good enough. Gas can be controlled; I can raise or lower the flame. But with coke a sudden little draft, more oxygen over the flame, more heat—and the side of the storeroom blows out. It happened. It makes the army very nervous. I told them I'd build a cellar and work in there. They said all right, if it blows, there's no damage done. 'Go ahead,' they said. 'It's your money.' And you came along just at the right time!"

When Slocum pressed down on the shovel, his knitted thighbone ached. Otherwise there was no reminder of the break. As for his project concerning the mad major, and the secondary project concerning the major's red-headed wife, he had decided that it was best to move very slowly, feeling his way like a cat walking along a shelf full of delicate china. The major was smart, cautious, and vigilant, and so were the people who surrounded him. Too many questions, too obvious an interest in the major and his movements, and someone would notice. They would start to take an interest in him, his background, and the places he had been. Someone might actually want to see what he looked like without a beard.

It was not too unlikely that a smart officer might come across the fact that he had escaped from the

## SLOCUM AND THE MAD MAJOR 121

territorial prison up in Wyoming. Or someone might come across that "Murderer Wanted" poster printed by the army in thousands after he had killed the Northern captain in New York State. Before he shot, he had made it very clear to the captain why he was being killed. The captain's wife had seen him and heard every word. The army had gotten his full description and record from the surrendered Confederate Army files. There was no statute of limitations on murder.

Slocum was suddenly aware of an unnatural silence. He leaned on the shovel and looked up. Mrs. Murray—he recognized her immediately by her striking red hair—was standing beside the pit. She wore a white, short-sleeved dress of fine muslin with a decorously scalloped neckline that gave a hint of her full breasts. Her red hair was coiled atop her head. A few wisps had escaped from the coil, and they trailed down her cheeks. Above her head she was idly twirling a small green silk parasol. She wore black shoes that reached to midcalf. She had very small, narrow feet. She stood calmly, waiting until Slocum finished his slow head-to-foot examination. He judged her to be a well-preserved thirty-five. In reality she was forty-two, but she had taken very good care of herself.

"Mrs. Murray, how do you do?" Johansen said, embarrassed by Slocum's direct stare at the woman.

He hoped that she would not be angry at the insolence. Johansen knew very little about women. He had no idea that attractive women like direct, sensual stares that coolly evaluate their bodies, particularly if they have fine bodies. Johansen did not offer to introduce Slocum. One did not introduce laborers to upper-class women. He was also embarrassed because of Slocum's naked upper torso.

Respectable women simply removed themselves from the presence of men without shirts. But she stood there, calmly surveying Slocum's heavily muscled body.

"I am fine, thank you," she replied.

Her voice, Slocum noticed, was a low, husky contralto.

"And who is digging out your new laboratory, Mr. Johansen?"

"Er, his name is Brian. Brian, put on your shirt."

Slocum turned to pick it up.

"Never mind, Brian. Are you Irish? I had an Irish wolfhound in Kansas named Brian Boru."

"No, ma'am." He did not like to be patronized, particularly by Major Murray's wife.

"Are you the man with the bear-claw necklace?" The parasol began to twirl.

"Yes, ma'am."

"You have very good pectoral muscles."

Slocum was silent.

"I draw, you know." She smiled. "I heard that you resented Corporal Morrissey's touching that necklace."

Slocum said nothing. She was amusing herself with a little light conversation, having nothing better to do this afternoon. She was the kind of upper-class woman who, Slocum was sure, found the enforced company of army wives dreadfully dull. And this would be especially so at a frontier post, far removed from the glitter and dazzle of San Francisco or New York.

Slocum did not know it, of course, but the woman's unhappiness constituted one of the strongest pressures upon the major to carry out his new policy of Apache raids.

"Well, Brian, you don't talk much. Just as well.

Perhaps one day you will pose for me. I am sick of drawing Indian squaws."

"Yes, ma'am."

"Not nude, of course—my husband would not approve—but wearing your famous necklace. Perhaps sitting down cross-legged on that bearskin I see inside the store?"

"Yes, ma'am."

"Is that the bear you killed with a knife?"

"Yes, ma'am."

She was clearly impressed, but she masked it with a light, mocking smile. "Well, then," she said briskly, "that's settled. Would that be all right with you, Mr. Johansen?"

Johansen did not like the idea at all. He was afraid that drawing sessions in his storeroom would start gossip. Then he would be placed in conflict with Major Murray, who would very likely want to know what kind of blasted stupidity was going on in the back of his store that the whole goddamn fort was sniggling over. The next step would be Major Murray seeing that he was expelled from the fort, right in the middle of his experiments.

But Johansen was afraid to say no to Mrs. Murray. She was the kind of woman who would make things hard for anyone who opposed her wishes.

"Sure." He nodded. "That's all right." He hoped that she would find a different toy to play with.

"Very well, then! It's settled. Now, Mr. Johansen, as you know, whenever Mr. Gompertz comes out here to see the major, I do not permit him in my house."

Johansen nodded. Slocum found this news mildly interesting. He continued to dig, his face impassive.

"So Gompertz and Major Murray will be coming

here, as usual. I'll send over some light refreshments for them. Shall we say at seven?"

"Yes, Mrs. Murray."

"Fine." She spun around and walked away without a backward glance.

Slocum leaned on his shovel and stared at her buttocks. Under the dress she was clearly naked; he was sure of that. The free jiggle and bounce of her breasts proved it. The rich sway of her buttocks seemed deliberately provocative. For the first time since Dilchay, Slocum felt a warmth building in his groin. She looked like a woman whom it would be a pleasure to dominate, and to humiliate. He had better not forget that.

"I don't like that woman," Johansen said. "She gives off a bad smell of trouble. And telling the major that he can't have a guest in his own house!" Johansen was scandalized. "That sure is a man who's pussy-whipped." He shook his head in disgust.

Slocum continued to dig. It would not do to show too much interest.

"Major's fault," he said. "Woman needs a good quirtin'."

"Ho, ho, ho, what have we here? A philosopher about women?"

Slocum shrugged.

"As a veteran of the marriage war, Brian," Johansen said, opening up a can of sardines and spearing one on his jackknife, "the more you live with women, the more you realize they're about as predictable as a bronc on a frosty morning. You know it's got something nasty lined up for you, but you don't know whether it'll sunfish, whipsaw, or just roll over on you and go to sleep. In other words, any philosopher worth his salt will say right off, 'I don't know a damn thing about the animals.'"

"Maybe."

Slocum was not convinced. At any rate, he didn't want to spend too much time thinking about Mrs. Murray. That would be like planning an expedition to shoot a woodchuck when there was a grizzly waiting around the bend of the trail. He smiled. If Mrs. Murray knew that he had just compared her to a woodchuck, she'd swell up so mad that she'd bust her corset laces. Then he remembered that she didn't wear corsets. The thought made him think of grinding his hips against hers.

One thing was sure. With that cool little smile of hers, she wouldn't be screwing like a woodchuck. She wouldn't just lie there like a New England spinster grimly subjecting herself to a disgusting, filthy man. It would be more like mating with a mountain lion in full heat. The thought of her slowly pulling up her green silk dress, with nothing underneath, just slowly pulling it up, up from her ankles, to her knees, to her thighs, till he could see the triangular patch of tightly curled red pubic hair—just the thought of it gave him a massive erection.

"Maybe I'm wrong," Slocum admitted. "But what's wrong with this Gompertz feller? Does he smell bad? Pass out with his head in the mashed potatoes?"

"No. They talk business. They just don't want her to listen, so she feels insulted. So she told the major that if she can't listen when he talks to that Gompertz fellow, they can't talk in *her* house and to go off elsewhere."

"How'd you know all this?"

"No way to keep a secret in this place with all those servants around. And that bodyguard keeps hanging around the house; she probably yelled at him. People listen and talk. They come here to kill time. They talk. I could even issue a gossip paper if I wanted. I hear *everything*. How about a spot of lemonade with bourbon?"

"*Lemonade?*"

Lemons came all the way from California. By the time they had been hauled in buckboards all the way up from the railroad, they brought three dollars apiece. Johansen squeezed out a couple of lemons and poured bourbon and a little cool water over the delicious blend.

They sat sipping quietly.

"When you finish digging for the day," Johansen said, "I'd like you to sweep out the store, wash the table, put on a clean tablecloth, clean the kerosene chimney, fill the lamp, and then clear out."

"Clear out?"

"It might be my place, but it's on army property. I don't fight hard."

"Can't we just go in the storeroom?"

Johansen smiled. "Murray sends his boys over first," he said. "They'll be here about six-thirty. They'll roust out any and all bystanders. That means you and me. They'll really go through that pile of Navajo blankets. Then a couple'll drape themselves over the porch, another two will hang around the back, and one man will take up a position on each side of the store."

"Murray ain't so popular, is he?"

Johansen grunted. "Why don't you wash up? You worked plenty hard enough for the day. I'll get the room ready. You just take it easy." He grabbed a broom and began sweeping, while Slocum washed himself in the basin and dried himself with the flour-bag towel.

As Johansen worked, he talked: "Right, Murray

isn't well liked around here ever since he stepped up those cavalry patrols. You bet your boots. A lot of the ranchers around here and even up to the rim think that all he'll accomplish by this crazy policy will be to stir up the ants. And the ants are going around biting everything they see. Before Murray started this patrol business, only an occasional ant did some biting. Maybe the ranchers are right. I sure as hell don't know. Once the Apaches held all this"—Johansen swung both arms in a broad sweep that took in the valley and the surrounding mountain ranges—"and then the Spaniards came. If the Apaches want to get even, they ought to go down to Mexico and kill Mexicans, right? Oh, it's all too complicated for a scientific mind. I like the simplicity of chemical reactions. Get your mixtures just right, and you get the same result each time. Want to fill the lamp? I've cleaned the chimney."

They worked in companionable silence. When everything was ready, Johansen said, "You'll have to wait outside till they're done. Sometimes Morrissey is on the bodyguard. Please be careful. I'm going to spend the night with a laundress down the line. Be back for breakfast. We'll have bacon and eggs. What say?"

"Sounds good."

"Wait till they leave before you go anywhere near the store. Stay out of trouble. Good night."

"Good night."

Johansen put on a jacket and left. The night was chilly. Slocum sat on the chair where Murray would be sitting. He imagined himself crouched under the table, invisible under the draped tablecloth, suddenly rising up and ramming Kazshe's knife into Murray's belly in the same way he had killed the grizzly. He sighed. No, it wouldn't work. Not with Murray's experienced bodyguard. He heard several men approaching. He stood up and peered through a window toward the officers' quarters. Walking across the parade ground came seven men. Three marched in front of the major, three in the rear. They were looking all around as they walked, their hands on their Colt butts. Slocum lit the lamp. He would like very much to listen to Murray's talk with Gompertz. But how could he? Where could he hide? Behind the counter? In the storeroom? Under the pile of Navajo blankets? Under the pile of furs? Behind the kerosene barrel?

The men reached the store. While the major waited outside, two men circled the store, hands on their gun butts, scanning the roof. The other four entered the store. One turned up the wick in the lamp to maximum illumination, took the lamp off the long hook that was suspended from the ceiling, and then walked through the storeroom. He was preceded by the other three men.

One of the men was Morrissey, who smiled at Slocum. As he walked by, he said, "We have to get together sometime, you and me, and sort of have a dance together."

The three men turned up the blankets and looked behind the barrels. One man picked up the broom and ran it along back of the counter. If anyone had been hiding there, he would have been flushed out. It was a good, tough, professional search.

Morrissey took the broom from him and swung it under the table. Then he pretended to start sweeping toward Slocum. Reaching Slocum's feet, he reared back in simulated surprise. "Goodness me! What have we here? A bedbug! A real big bedbug, by God!"

The sergeant walked in. "Enough of that, you fool," he said harshly. "I don't want no mess made of this room with the major waiting just outside. As for you," he added, turning toward Slocum and jerking his thumb, "out!"

Slocum was mindful of Johansen's request for peace. He walked into the storeroom, took a Navajo blanket, and walked out, disregarding Morrissey's jeering grin. He walked past the sentry on the porch, past the impassive Major Murray, who gave him a casual, bored look, and continued into the scrub chaparral behind the store. After finding a small hollow, he put the blanket over himself, and pretended to go to sleep. He knew that he was being observed.

Time passed. The light faded. Someone lit the kerosene lamp. The yellow windows glowed in the darkness. Murray stepped outside on the porch and lit a cigar; he paced restlessly back and forth. Slocum slid out of the blanket. He broke off several clumps of *sacaton* grass and stuffed them into the folded blanket. It now looked as if a sleeping man were inside it. He was ready for some eavesdropping if chance put something his way.

A buckboard suddenly rattled into the fort. A man sat beside the driver, bundled up in a heavy overcoat. Two heavily armed riders rode in front, and two rode in back. Murray threw away his cigar and walked impatiently toward the buckboard. Slocum writhed quickly toward the edge of the parade ground and found a small pile of discarded chairs waiting to be hauled away to the fort dump. He lay flat behind them. The buckboard came to a halt fifteen feet away.

Slocum could not hear Murray's first few words.

He heard Gompertz say, "I'm sorry you feel that way, Murray."

"I'm tired of having a messenger run back and forth carrying messages," Murray replied. He was clearly in a rotten mood. He lit another cigar. "I also don't like being called by my last name by a messenger either. No wonder Mrs. Murray won't have you in the house. She has a sensitive nose."

"Now look here—"

Murray paid no attention. "Now, Gompertz, you go on back to Tucson. When you get there, you tell Bailey that I've stuck to my share of the bargain. I've stirred them up, and they're doing what I want them to do. And you know what, Gompertz? I don't see any return favors. I don't see any letters."

Gompertz said mildly, "He doesn't write letters."

"So what *does* he do? He sends you! I put up with it for a while, but it's not enough! You go back and tell him I want to talk to *him* and not to an errand boy. Nothing personal, Gompertz. My wife is giving me hell because I'm still stationed out here. I promised her that two months would see us back in Michigan. That was months ago!"

"I will see what I can do, Major," Gompertz said in his mild voice.

He took Murray by the left elbow. Murray jerked it away. He hated to be touched.

"I don't want you to see what you can do. I want him here Tuesday night at seven. That's final. If he doesn't come, why, he'll be very, very sorry, because I'll just dump everything down the drain."

Gompertz was silent.

"That's clear now, isn't it?"

"Yes. I'll have him here at nine. He doesn't like people seeing him."

"Nine will do," Murray said, satisfied. "I'd have

him in my house, but by now Mrs. Murray is sick of all you people and sick of all the long talks. So we'll be meeting in the post trader's. He can be sure of absolute privacy. Is there anything particular he likes to eat?"

"Soft-boiled eggs and fresh goat's milk, please."

Murray laughed in contempt. "The richest man in Arizona! He could eat quail eggs and truffles and drink champagne!"

"Yes. However, his stomach limits him to this rigorous diet."

"I suppose I could rustle up some greaser around here with a couple of goats. He'll have his damn goat's milk. Jesus!"

"I'll tell him, Major. I'm sure he will appreciate this courtesy."

"Tell him," the major began angrily. Then he stopped. "Oh, hell. It can wait. Good night."

"Good night, Major."

Gompertz walked toward his waiting buckboard. The major strode furiously toward his house on the other side of the parade ground. Slocum lay there and thought. He wanted to listen to the conversation that would be held in the store next Tuesday evening, and suddenly he knew how he could do it. He watched Murray move, followed and preceded by his ever-vigilant escort. When everyone had disappeared, he got up, walked over to his blanket, shook out the *sacaton*, and headed back to the storeroom. He unhooked the lantern and hung it up inside. Piled helter-skelter in a dark, dusty corner were odds and ends of lumber, ranging in size from two by fours to flooring. On one wall was a neatly arranged tool rack. On the wall Johansen had drawn the outline of each tool, each hammer, each plane, each screwdriver. The arrangement of nails on which the tools were hung, supported, or braced looked wildly arbitrary, if the viewer were simply to look at the nails and nothing else. But once the outline had been drawn around each tool, it became the simplest thing in the world to return each one to its proper place. This fascinated Slocum, who wondered why he found such a basically simple thing so interesting.

"Ah!" he said aloud. "That's it!"

All the things that Murray had done to the Chiricahua had been puzzling. There was no pattern that he could understand. Why had the major deliberately attacked a small and relatively peaceful band? Even if Nachodise could not be considered a kindly fellow, why kill all the women and children? That was simply poor strategy, and Murray had proved in the war that he was a fine strategist. Good strategy here called for a talk with the leader of the band, whoever he might be. There had to be an attempt to work out a peaceful solution. That's what soldiers were for. If peace was not possible, a soldier went to war. If a war party had gone out and come back flourishing scalps, all the more reason to seek out just those who were personally guilty. Civilized soldiers did not wipe out the women and children of the members of a war party. How did the army expect to bring peace and security to a lawless Indian frontier if such a savage policy were followed? It made no sense.

It made no sense, that is, unless it was part of a deliberate policy by the major to force every Apache in Arizona onto the warpath: the Chiricahua, the San Carlos, the White Mountain, and maybe the Mescalero eastward in New Mexico. The talk the major would be having on Tuesday night might make the whole pattern clear.

Slocum took a pile of assorted lumber out of the storeroom and set it in the cellar he had been digging behind the store. Then he blew out the lamp. He wanted any casual or suspicious observer to think that he had gone to bed. He was going to work in the dark out back, but the quarter moon would yield enough light for what he was going to do. He jumped into the hole. In two hours he had shoveled out enough dirt to make a tunnel that should reach just under the table where Murray and Gompertz's boss would be sitting. As he dug, he braced the tunnel with planks for a roof and two by fours for uprights.

When Slocum had finished that, he crawled out backward and went into the storeroom. He found some maple dowels that were twelve inches long and half an inch in diameter. They would work just fine. Next he selected a half-inch drill. Enough moonlight was coming in through the window. He moved the table aside and drilled a hole in the floor, just where the center of the table would be when it was in its proper place. He rubbed soap all down the length of the dowel, set it in the hole, and pounded it down gently with his closed fist. It sank in smoothly because of the soap. When the dowel was flush with the floor, he took the broom and swept dust back and forth over the pale brown end of the dowel. A keen eye searching hard for something unusual would spot it right away. But it would be under the table, in the shadow cast by the table. Slocum was sure that it would be safe enough.

He went back into the hole and shoveled dirt into the tunnel opening until it was full. Then he patted it with the flat of the shovel until it looked just like the other sides of the cellar. He took back the unused lumber. Satisfied with the night's work, he lay down on the pile of Navajo blankets and went to sleep immediately.

When Johansen opened the door to the storeroom and the light poured in, Slocum came to his feet instantly.

"Holy cow," Johansen told him, "you move like a cat!"

Slocum said nothing. He was annoyed with himself for sleeping too hard. If Johansen had been an Apache or even a drunken Morrissey looking to get even, Slocum would have been dead.

"I had a rough night," Johansen informed him. "She wouldn't let me alone." He groaned, went outside and filled a washpan from the rain barrel. With much blowing and puffing, he washed. He wiped his face with a crudely stitched, coarse flour sack. "My wife would die if she saw this towel," he said, holding it aloft. "Now you just look at it! It's got a big beautiful stalk of golden wheat right smack in the middle. And what's wrong with wiping yourself with 'Junius Whittaker and Sons Flour Millers St. Paul Minnesota'? It looks real nice." He hung it on its nail. "And now, breakfast!"

He made bacon and eggs while Slocum washed.

"Today we'll finish digging out the new Johansen Laboratory," Johansen said.

After breakfast, Slocum began digging again. By noon he had finished. While he was eating lunch, a few soldiers came in. Over their sardines and crackers, they began the endless cavalry debate of saber versus revolver. It still goes on, Slocum thought, smiling. He had dropped the saber from his own command early in the war. The weapon was always banging against the poor horses' flanks or slapping the riders' legs. The men didn't keep it sharp; it got rusty. If a man lifted it for a down stroke, a better man would slip in the point. Or an opponent could simply move back ten feet and shoot him in comfort. It did have some use as the symbol of the cavalryman; it was fine for parades. If a man had run out of ammunition, the saber could be useful. But no one got enough practice at it to use it really effectively. When Slocum thought about it, all in all, it was just a relic from the days before gunpowder. It was about as useful as an appendix.

Morrissey came in. He had heard the tail end of the discussion. "It's me for the saber, boys!" he said. "They don't like the point. So I say, give them the point! It can be very discouragin' for a Chiricahua to look down and see a saber hilt restin' against his breastbone. Makes a man want to go home and think things over a bit afore he gets on a horse and goes out to lift hair or somethin'. What say, Bearclaw?"

The others tittered. Slocum realized that this must be his nickname. It could have been worse.

"No," he said. He carefully scraped the last of the bacon and beans from his plate.

"What do you mean, no?" Morrissey, drunk or sober, didn't like to be argued with.

"Problem is gettin' the saber into the breastbone. Man has to get close. He has to have the point real sharp. He has to drive it home in the right place. It's awful hard to do from the back of a horse, especially with that noise bangin' all around."

"You been in the war?"

It was time to leave this dangerous topic. These were the soldiers of the victorious Northern army. He always kept in mind the fact that they would go after anyone who had shot down one of their own. Slocum had killed that Northern officer after the war had ended. That meant that it was not an act of war—it was murder. And a Northern jury would not be kind. People had resentments and long memories after a civil war.

"Yes," he said shortly.

"What side?"

That was a dangerous question. The war had been over for fifteen years, but that meant nothing. And he knew that his accent had a Southern tinge.

"South." And he added, to blunt any resentment, "Engineers."

No one hated engineers. Engineers never killed anybody. They built bridges and repaired torn-up railroad tracks.

"Ing-gin-eeers!" Morrissey said mockingly. "Real safe, wasn't it, Bearclaw?"

Johansen turned from the stove where he had been making coffee. "Morrissey," he said, patiently, "I'm getting tired of having you come in here and pick fights. Now, you're a bigger and stronger man than I am, but if you don't shut up and stop trying to start up with my help, I'm going right to Captain Sibley. He'll see that this place is off limits to you. What do you say?"

Morrissey flushed. Finally, with his voice sullen and his face filled with hate, he said, "All right. But what happens outside ain't got nothin' to do with you. Now give me a couple of them cigars. And here's money!"

He banged a silver dollar on the counter and Johansen served him courteously. Morrissey rammed the cigars into his left blouse pocket and stood indecisively. Slocum watched him calmly as he spooned up the last of his beans. The man was searching for something to say that would allow him to leave without seeming to have been run out.

The sudden entrance of Mrs. Murray saved him. Under her left arm she held a large sketch pad. "Good morning, men," she said.

"Mornin', ma'am," they mumbled, pulling off their caps.

"Mr. Johansen," she said, "I'll need several pencils."

The men filed out. Slocum went into the new laboratory to work. An hour passed.

Johansen came by. "I've got a nag in the stables," he said. "Her name's Dolly. It's getting too hot out here to do any work. Why don't you look Dolly up? Get acquainted! Tell the sergeant down there I said it's all right. The saddle is back of her stall—saddle blanket, all the gear. Murray planned that stable very well. You'll see. Got to give the man credit."

Slocum's curiosity was aroused. He strolled over to the stable. This was the first time he had been close to it, and he looked at it carefully. It was a long frame building. There was an opening along each side of the ridge for ventilation. At the head of each stall was a tin placard with the number of the horse, its name, the name of its rider, and the number of its rider. Underneath the placard was a roller of salt. Murray had invented it; it was for the horse to lick. At the rear of the stalls, the saddles were hung from wooden hooks. Each saddle was covered with its own piece of canvas. Inside each stall was a small canvas bag holding a curry comb and brush.

Slocum walked along the aisles, looking for Dolly's placard.

"What the hell you want?" Morrissey demanded. He came out of a stall with a placard that read "Fatima," the Major's pure-bred Arabian mare. In his hand Morrissey held a curry comb.

"Looking."

"Well," Morrissey said with pleasure, "you can't look here. Go somewhere's else and look. Because I'm the boyo who says who looks here and who don't. And I don't want a flea-bitten fur trapper hangin' around the major's horses."

Slocum was getting tired of Morrissey. He took a long, slow deep breath. It was his way of counting to ten before he took an irreversible step.

"Johansen told me to give Dolly a run."

"Yeah? I don't believe it."

Very quietly Slocum asked, "You callin' me a liar?"

Morrissey realized that he had gone too far. He reached behind himself for a pitchfork.

"Corporal!"

"Yes, ma'am."

"I couldn't help overhearing your last remark."

She had come in quietly. She was wearing a long riding skirt and boots. In her right hand she held a quirt.

"Yes, ma'am." He stared sullenly at the floor.

"Or is it private again?"

"Private, ma'am."

"I thought so. Will you be good enough to go to my house and tell Antonia I forgot my straw riding hat? The one with the green ribbon, please."

"But the major told me—"

She smashed her quirt against the boards of the

stall with such violence that Dolly jumped. Several horses turned their heads.

"Do it! And without arguments!"

Morrissey flushed.

"I'll take care of any complaints from that end," she said, her voice suddenly soft and relaxed again.

Slocum thought that these sudden uncontrollable rages, alternating with calms just as sudden, must put terrible pressures upon her husband.

"If you say so, ma'am."

"I say so." She stared at him, not winking.

Morrissey hesitated, and then he shrugged. He leaned the pitchfork back against the wall and walked out.

"Disgusting man," she said.

Slocum said nothing. He had been petting Dolly. The horse kept nuzzling him, hoping for the lump of sugar that Johansen always provided. Slocum threw the saddle blanket over Dolly. He unhooked the saddle and dropped it on her back. He pulled the cinches tight.

"You throw that saddle on as if it were a feather."

"Yes, ma'am."

He reached for the bit.

"And you are very skillful around horses. What did you do before you were a mountain man?"

She sat down on a crude bench, crossed her legs, and tapped the toe of one boot with her quirt.

"Punched cows."

"That's not much of a specialty in Arizona. And before?"

"Different things. Here and there."

"Mountain men don't talk much, do they?" She stood up and crossed her arms. The gesture pushed her breasts upward. "Have you met my husband?"

"Seen him."

"He's out today on one of those patrols of his." She swung her quirt at the stall. Dolly jumped again. Two stalls away, a nervous horse violently kicked his stall. "That's a wild mustang," she said.

Slocum looked with interest. Wild mustangs never wound up in stables.

"One of the officers caught it a couple of days ago," she said. "Back there somewhere." She pointed the quirt toward the ridge. "It had a wrenched knee and couldn't run. He says he's going to tame it. What do you think about that?"

"Mustangs are only wolf bait. Too small, too scrawny. Can't carry a heavy man."

"That's what I told the young fool. But Carter says he can break it and prove they can be good cavalry horses. He says the army should use horses native to the territory." She mocked the phrase. "He says it all the time and stares at me with those big round eyes." She shook her head in irritation. "Ah, well," she added in one of her sudden shifts of mood, "we were all young once." She got up and walked to the mustang's stall. "There, there," she said soothingly. "There, there." The sound calmed the wild horse. His ears moved slowly erect from their flattened position.

"My, my," Mrs. Murray said suddenly. "Look at *that!*"

Slocum looked. He could see nothing. He led Dolly out of her stall.

"Good *Lord!*"

Slocum looked where she was pointing. The mustang had produced a huge erection that was shining red and slick. Dolly had excited him. As Slocum brought Dolly alongside the mustang, he got a stronger whiff of Dolly, and his penis swelled even more. Mrs. Murray flushed with excitement.

"Will you look at that," she whispered. Then she turned her head and stared at Slocum.

He was sure that if he were to push her back onto a bale of hay beside the stall, she would not resist in the slightest. She squeezed her thighs together and took a deep, quivering breath. Her color had heightened even more. Her breathing speed had increased. Slocum thought that she looked like a woman who was being made love to.

"When I was a child," she said, speaking quickly and nervously, "we went to a farm for the summer. Back in Michigan. They had a mare. They didn't know I was in the hayloft. They brought in a stallion. It was very puzzling to me and very exciting. The mare kicked and whinnied. The stallion mounted her. I thought she was being hurt, but the farmer was a nice man, and I knew he wouldn't do anything to hurt Queenie. Maybe it did hurt her, but I know now she must have been enjoying it, too. God, wouldn't Dolly like that big thing inside her!"

She turned to Dolly and stroked her velvety soft muzzle. "Wouldn't you, Dolly?" she crooned. "Wouldn't you like that big, long thing inside you, ramming you hard? Oh, Dolly, you know you would, you just know you would." She looked at Slocum while she was talking. "Wouldn't she just *love* it, Bearclaw? Wouldn't she—"

Morrissey walked in. In his big right hand he was holding her hat with the green ribbon. He walked up and handed it to her. She looked distastefully at his grimy hand and took the hat.

"Thank you," she said coolly. "Would you be good enough to saddle the mare for me."

"Yes'm."

Slocum led Dolly out of the stable. He felt both their stares. It looked as if there might be some movement very soon with his Mrs. Murray project.

After he had ridden Dolly for an hour and gradually increasing her rather bored amble into a reluctant trot and then into a canter, Slocum walked her across the chaparral flat behind the parade ground to a thick, dense stand of cottonwood at the edge of the river. It was very cool in the grove, very soothing after the hot, violent glare of the merciless sun. It was silent, except for the furious *rat-a-tat-tat* of a big red-crested woodpecker feverishly searching for grubs. The ground was littered with dried twigs, dead branches, and the damp, accumulated leaf fall of years.

Dolly began munching the poplar-shaped cottonwood leaves. In wintertime, when there was no other food, it was possible to stay alive by eating the inner bark of the trees. Slocum had done it once up in the Bitter Roots. He did not look back on that winter with any fondness. He stripped off Dolly's saddle and draped the blanket over a horizontal bough that stretched fifteen feet over the brown river. He stripped himself naked and led Dolly into the water. She was reluctant, and he had to urge her. Probably, he thought, she had never seen a river as anything but something large, wet, and dangerous, which her riders had wanted her to cross for some inexplicable reason.

He took Dolly in to her knees. He curried her with a handful of leaves, sloshing her frequently with double handfuls of water. She enjoyed that. After he had washed off her sweat, he led her ashore and tied her. He went back, ducked a few times, and scrubbed himself with handfuls of dried leaves. When he was wading ashore again, he saw Morrissey leaning against a tree with his arms folded.

"You ain't much of a mountain man," Morrissey said with his perpetual sneer. "If I was a Chiricahua, you would have been dead twice over."

Slocum wiped himself dry with his shirt. He paid no attention to Morrissey, who continued to watch him narrowly.

"For a fellow who's a mountain man, you got yourself shot up a little too much looks like."

Slocum reached for his drawers. Dolly nuzzled him in a friendly manner.

"Got a nice big hole there in your leg. Looks pretty damn new, don't it?"

Slocum pulled on his pants.

"A *big* hole. Looks like a .45-50 Springfield bullet to me. My weapon, Mr. Bearclaw."

Slocum pulled on his boots. He pushed Dolly away. She was nuzzling him harder, looking for sugar.

"Funny-lookin' scar around it. Like you tried to get at the bullet yourself. Must have been no doctors around."

Slocum buttoned his shirt.

"I think I shot some white renegade in the leg up back there two, three months ago. Couldn't swear who it was. Man didn't have a beard. Man can grow one if he wants, though. Like to see you all shaved. What say, Bearclaw?"

Slocum threw Dolly's saddle blanket over her.

"Sure wasn't no doctors up there, right?"

Slocum threw the saddle on and cinched it. Morrissey came very close then to being killed and having his body rolled into the brown flood. The current would have taken his body away from the fort. It would have taken days before it surfaced again, somewhere along the course of the Gila. But two things held Slocum back: He didn't want to leave until he had taken care of the major, and he didn't want to steal Dolly from the man who had entrusted her to his care.

He mounted Dolly.

"See you around," Morrissey said, grinning. His hands were still in his pockets.

Slocum thought that only a fool would make such dangerous remarks with his hands in his pockets. Getting them out in a hurry would take a precious half second.

"You bet you will," Slocum said softly. He rode away.

## 16

Bailey sipped from his daily glass of goat's milk. As he put the glass down, he made a wry face. He leaned back, hooking his thumbs into his vest pockets.

"What did our friend say?" he asked.

Gompertz shrugged. "He isn't having any talk from a messenger."

"That's what he called you?" Bailey asked with a smile.

"Yes."

"You don't look insulted."

"Isn't that what I am? A highly paid one, but a messenger all the same." Gompertz sat with his hands clasped together on the round mahogany table. The table was so carefully and lavishly waxed that his face seemed to float on it.

"Yes," Bailey said. "That's what you are. But you mean you're *really* not insulted?"

"Why should I be?" With his clasped hands Gompertz looked like a prim schoolteacher. "I am a man who makes no pretensions. I do what I do. I do it well."

"You don't even feel a *little* mad?"

Gompertz smiled. "No."

Bailey shook his head and drank more milk. "I guess I'll never really understand you, Gompertz. If he said that to me, I might have punched him."

"You would punch an army major on his own ground?"

"Sure would."

Gompertz nodded. "Yes, you might. You'd be shoved into the guardhouse overnight, but you'd be out soon enough."

"That's true." Bailey grinned. "What good is money and influence if I can't get to use them, hey?" He finished the goat's milk, made another face, and shoved the glass aside.

"Now, Gompertz, I got a deal cooking up in Flagstaff. I—"

"Our friend wants to see you."

"He'll have to do what they all have to do: wait his turn. I don't jump for *anyone* any more. People jump for me. You can tell him that. But be nice."

"If he doesn't see you, he'll spill the beans."

Bailey's eyes opened wide for a second. Then his eyelids lowered. It was his way of showing serious concern, Gompertz knew.

"He knows an awful lot of important beans," Gompertz said in his calm, level voice.

Bailey was getting angry. "Does he have any idea what it takes to line up all the party bosses so they'll get behind his nomination and push? Does he have any goddamn idea of all the promises and favors I have to hand out not only in this goddam territory but also in Washington? Does he know how long all that takes? Does he know how many companies I'm running here? Does he know I travel around buying cattle? Take trains to Chicago and Omaha, making stockyard deals? Does he—oh, shit, Gompertz, I'll just have to go or the whole goddamn thing might blow up in my face."

"It would be best."

"Make arrangements."

"Yes. I think all he needs is soothing noises. He'll probably take them from you but not from a messenger. You have an appointment for Tuesday at nine."

"You're a smart man, Gompertz."

"Yes, sir."

"I'm very lucky this isn't just a job I have working for some big company. You'd make me very nervous."

"Yes, sir."

"But since I'm the boss, I have nothing to worry about. Line up a buggy and a strong escort."

"I've already ordered eight men down from the ranch up on Las Animas. They're coming down with that new Studebaker buggy."

"And no doubt you told Murray to set out some goat's milk!"

"Yes."

"I figured as much. Let him get his complaining over with. There's too much riding on him. Millions. *Millions*. You know, I just thought of something. That wife of his, that red-headed bitch. He might want to be governor of the territory so much, he might loan her to me from time to time. What's your opinion?"

"Within the bounds of possibility, sir."

"Well, then, we'll have to make sure he gets to be governor, won't we?"

# 17

The next morning Major Murray led a patrol. The two Pima scouts rode ahead. The road led south through the flat country at the western end of the valley. It was mostly low chaparral, with a few saguaros scattered irregularly through the desert country like huge candelabra. Cactus wrens flitted in and out of holes in the thick, fleshy stems, bringing grasshoppers to their tiny, wide-mouthed fledglings.

An occasional coyote loped easily across the road and sat down at the edge, watching the horses go by. The coyotes' constant curiosity and vigilance and their red lolling tongues intrigued Sibley. They always seemed to be vastly amused at something. It was probably, Sibley thought, because when they let their tongues hang out, they looked as if they were smiling. And maybe they were.

He said as much to Lieutenant Carter,

"Vermin," Carter replied. "They're vermin. They kill calves; they kill lambs. Ought to kill them all."

"Well," Sibley said, "I just don't know about that. They kill a calf or a lamb once in a while, that's true. But what they mostly eat are the old or sick cows and sheep. And why shouldn't they?"

"I don't know what you're talking about," Carter said curtly. He had already picked up Murray's brusque way of talking to Sibley. If the major treated Sibley with impatience, Carter would damn well imitate him.

Sibley smiled at that. "Permit me to make myself clear," he said calmly.

"Oh, Jesus," Carter said under his breath but loud enough for Sibley to hear.

Sibley chose to disregard the remark. He was always tolerant of people's weaknesses. The men of his company never minded coming before him for punishment. His reputation for leniency was well deserved.

Carter unscrewed his canteen and took a long drink. Sibley waited. He saw no reason to point out that they were heading for dry, stony mountain trails where water was scarce. A man ought to have sense enough to drink all the water he could hold before riding out of the fort on a hot day. One thing was sure—he would let the shavetail find out the hard way. That would take some of that arrogance out of him and leave him with a good, powerful impression about being sensible with water. Sibley decided that he wasn't going to give the stupid kid any of his water.

"Coyotes eat prairie dogs, snakes, mice, all sorts of things," Sibley continued after Carter had screwed the canteen cap back on. "Now, opening up all this country to cattle wiped out a lot of the prairie dog population. When they brought in sheep, those buggers grazed so close that the mice couldn't make nests any more. What's a poor coyote going to do for breakfast? Suppose, Carter, suppose someone came into your house and busted all the nice pickled beets in your pantry. Just walked in without any introduction and busted all those glass jars all filled with string beans, stewed tomatoes, corn. Ruined your winter food supply."

Sibley was used to conversations like this on the road with companionable, friendly fellow officers. It passed the time and took their minds off the heat, which was coming down at them like a fiery sledgehammer. Ropes of foam began to form at the corners of the horses' mouths. Occasionally a horse would shake his head, and the foam would fly off and land on Sibley's pants. He paid no attention. Carter, on the other hand, let out an involuntary yelp of disgust. Ah, thought Sibley, wait till a man's brains get blown all over the kid's face. Let's see how he'll handle *that*.

Carter undid the knot of his bandana, rolled it into a cylinder, and tied it around his neck so that it would absorb his sweat more efficiently.

"Young Mr. Carter!"

Carter jumped at Major Murray's peremptory tone. Murray was riding in the middle of the column of fours, preceded and followed by his ever-present bodyguard. They were always well turned-out. Sibley smiled to himself. The major's eyes were very sharp, and he liked a spit-and-polish look on everyone.

"Sir!"

"Be so good as to remember that you are an officer and a gentleman, by act of Congress. Gentlemen wear their bandanas properly. Not like a Mexican teamster. See to it."

Several men tittered. The red-faced lieutenant muttered, "Yes, sir." He untied the bandana, shook it out, and then retied and redraped it in the correct cavalry manner.

"The old man sees everything," Sibley said kindly. Then, to change the topic and relieve Carter's embarrassment, he added, "Back to coyotes."

"Must we?" Carter groaned.

"We must," Sibley said firmly.

Carter unscrewed his canteen and took another drink.

One of the bodyguard cantered up. "Major's compliments, sir!"

"What is it, Weiss?"

"Sir, the major said for you to tell the lieutenant to go easy on the water. Sir, he said you should have told him that the first time he took a drink."

"All right, Weiss."

The man cantered back.

"I said the old man saw *everything*," Sibley continued. "Do you want the canteen lecture or the coyote lecture?"

"I'm in for both of them, I see that. Better tell me first about canteens. When you finish that, I'll just have to listen to you go on about your coyotes, won't I?"

"I suppose you will," Sibley said gently. He began the water lecture.

Three miles from the fort, the road entered a small, narrow defile that was two hundred yards long. Thousands of years ago it had been an arroyo, carved twenty feet deep into the sandstone by a river. Long afterward the river had had its headwaters blocked by a landslide that came down the west face of Dzil Ligai. As a result, the river abandoned its old bed and now ran westward into the San Pedro. All of this had happened before the Apaches had drifted down that way from the Bering Strait.

The arroyo—now a narrow little canyon—was a natural place for an ambush. Indeed, it was called Brown's Canyon in memory of the man who had been ambushed, tortured, and killed there twenty years before. Every traveler and every Apache knew it.

On top of the canyon, low scrub chaparral grew along each side in the clay soil. As the column neared the canyon, it slowed automatically. Sibley held up a hand, and the column halted. They waited patiently for the Pima scouts to conduct their examination before they split apart. Each man climbed to the top of the ledge bordering Brown's Canyon. Then they rode along it. They rode to the end of the canyon, halted, and waved for the column to move ahead. Sibley let out a sigh of relief. He especially hated ambushes early in the day.

Murray rode silently. The bodyguard was also silent. They had seen him go through a personality change during the past four months. Before that he had been amiable; he had been tolerant about singing in the ranks and chatter so long as silence on the march was not an essential part of a planned attack.

Lately he had been putting on weight, mostly as a result of his heavy drinking. People would talk to him, and he would stare at them and nod from time to time. Then it would become clear that he had not the faintest recollection of what had been said.

Sibley, who functioned as Murray's executive officer, had been able to cover himself by writing out most of his suggestions and having Murray write "approved" or "not approved," followed by his initials. Requests from Murray were immediately written down by Sibley and given a date; the action taken was dutifully noted. His long army experience let Sibley know that this was the only possible way to cover himself against any future denial by Murray that he had not ordered such a thing.

Sibley felt that Murray's change of personality dated from the early visits of the civilian named Gompertz from Tuscon. It was a puzzle, to say the least.

Once out of Brown's Canyon, everyone relaxed. The road ran straight through flat, unappetizing country once more. The land tilted upward, filled with dead juniper and burnt-out tamarisk where lightning had started a fire the year before. Yucca and ocotillo flourished. Then the land pitched upward in an even steeper climb. Pinyons appeared first as stragglers and then became massed together up to the crest of the ridges. No ambush could be launched from such areas; they were too far from the road. It was time to resume the coyote lecture, Sibley decided.

"To continue, Carter," Sibley began. "Someone's come into your house and smashed up your food supply, and put *his* glass jars in your pantry. Different kinds of food from what you've been used to eating but still good to eat. So, you eat away."

"And the coyotes are eating now in our pantry?"

"Yes."

"I think you're ridiculous."

"And they're doing us a favor, too," Sibley said calmly.

"A *favor*!"

"Yes. Consider this, Carter. They'll eat an occasional lamb or calf, true. But what they eat mostly are the weak and the sick or the lame. By culling that way, they prevent the weakness and the sickness from being bred into the herds. They are actually improving the stock, and at very little expense to the ranchers."

"Oh, yes? Captain, I beg to differ—" He stopped abruptly.

The column had halted at Sibley's uplifted right hand. He had seen the Pima scouts racing their scrawny Indian ponies toward the column. They braked to a halt opposite Murray's position in the middle of the column. Murray's face became alive. Sibley turned in the saddle and watched. The Pimas were talking rapidly in Spanish. Murray frowned and held up a hand, cutting off the flow of words.

Murray beckoned Sibley close. Sibley trotted up.

"What's he saying?" Murray demanded. "It's too fast for me."

Sibley turned to the scouts. The spokesman began to talk. Murray fretted while Sibley listened intently. He combed his thick mustache with his riding glove and tapped nervously on the pommel. He looked back and forth along the ridges, but all he saw were the contorted shapes of wind-blasted junipers.

"Well, Sibley?"

"He's not finished, sir. It looks important."

"Damn it, tell him to get on with it and stop any bullshit Great Spirit talk. Jesus Christ Almighty!"

The Pimas looked blankly at Murray. They knew he was cursing and could not understand why. No Indian ever interrupted another.

*"Hable más, amigo mio,"* Sibley said soothingly. "Keep on talking, my friend."

Reassured, the Pima went on. When he had finished, he rested both hands on the pommel and waited patiently as Sibley translated. Murray jerked his head at Sibley and rode off several yards into the chaparral. He wanted privacy. The men were tense and silent, watching them narrowly.

"Go ahead," Murray said.

"They struck a trail crossing the road up ahead. There were twelve Apaches; three stolen horses, the rest Indian ponies. One horse carried two men. The horses were fresh. The trail is about twenty minutes old."

Murray and Sibley had learned from long frontier experience never to question the Pima scouts and their uncanny ability to read sign. Things like a sharp edge on a hoof print, the number of grains of sand that had fallen into it since the print was made, the wind direction, one or two stalks of crushed grass slowly becoming erect—all these were as obvious to a Pima as a letter would be to a white man.

"Where are they heading?"

"Toward Diamond Mesa."

"Do the scouts know why?"

"Yes, the Colcord ranch, most likely."

"Was it a war party?"

"Yes. All men, riding fast."

"How far to the ranch?"

Sibley had already taken the map from his pouch. He unfolded it. "Four miles."

"How many people live on the ranch?"

Sibley turned to the scouts and asked them the question in Spanish. They answered without hesitation. He turned back to Murray. "Mr. and Mrs.

Colcord, three children, a Mexican maid, and ten cowpunchers. They say the men are well-armed."

"Do you realize what you're telling me, Sibley? You're saying that this war party of twelve men is going to attack ten well-armed cowpunchers. I don't believe it! Your Pimas are getting feeble-minded. Maybe it's the heat."

Sibley turned and spoke briefly to the scout. The scout answered promptly.

"He says the cowpunchers are all down at the far end of the ranch, behind Oxbow Mountain, digging out a tank. The tank is about fifteen miles from the ranch house. They've been digging it for about seven, eight days."

Murray stroked his mustache and brooded. Sibley waited patiently for Murray to order the company to follow the war party as quickly as possible.

"Wait here, Sibley," Murray said. "I don't believe them." He thought for a moment. Then he came to a decision. He beckoned to the scouts. The bodyguard automatically began to follow them. "No!" Murray said sharply. "Stay here."

The men were puzzled, but they obeyed. Murray and the two Pimas rode off at a lope. A quarter of a mile ahead, one of the scouts pointed downward at the war party's trail. Sibley saw Murray nodding in response. Then the three riders left the road and climbed upward. Once at the ridge, they were outlined against the sky for a second. Then they disappeared.

Sibley sat his horse silently. He tried to puzzle out the situation and what it meant. Murray, Sibley knew, had no reason at all to doubt the Pimas. They had never made a mistake. They were brave men and would have absolutely no hesitation about following the trail of their old enemies.

Had Sibley been in command, he would have ridden hard after the Apaches. After all, a hard-riding patrol would have a decent chance of overtaking a group that was moving at a trot, especially on a trail that was only half an hour old. And the Pimas had no doubt whatsoever that the Apaches were on their way to attack the Colcord ranch.

Well, Sibley thought, there was no reason to sit their horses and tire them by waiting. He ordered the men to dismount but to keep their relative positions.

Lieutenant Carter said with shining eyes, "Not many commanders would act as their own scouts, eh?"

"No," Sibley answered dryly.

He did not add that intelligent commanders picked reliable scouts and trusted them. And why didn't Murray take his bodyguard along? That was very puzzling. He found a large rock near the road and sat in its shade while he held his horse's reins. The horse nosed disconsolately at the sparse vegetation.

"He's a very brave man," Carter went on.

And I think he's insane, Sibley mused silently. What in hell is he up to?

"Keep a sharp lookout, you men!" he called out. "This is Apache country, and don't you ever forget it."

Carter stuck his hands in his pockets and began a tuneless whistling.

"Stop that racket, will you!" Sibley snapped, and was immediately sorry. Carter bit his lip and was silent.

An hour later, three horses appeared at the top of the ridge.

"Prepare to mount! Mount!" Sibley ordered. Murray and the scouts trotted down to the patrol. To Sibley's questioning, he only shook his head.

"Bad, *bad*," he said. "We will follow the scouts."

The scouts took their old path, following the Apache trail. At the ridge the trail went down and then followed the course of a small valley around Mailbox Mesa. On the far side was the Colcord ranch. A column of smoke was rising vertically from the ranch house in the windless air. Even at the distance of half a mile Sibley could see the motionless shapes lying in the front yard. He counted six. That took care of the Colcords, their children, and the Mexican maid.

The war party's trail led up the valley from the ranch house. Then it disappeared into some *malpais*. The scouts had cantered ahead. The trail petered out into the lava beds of the *malpais*. There was no way to follow a trail through that kind of surface, as Sibley and Murray well knew.

The dead lay lanced or knifed. Inside, the house was a shambles. They had emptied Mrs. Colcord's bureau and hope chest and scattered her dresses and linen everywhere. The flour barrel had been tipped over, and bloody footprints were tracked all over the floor. Colcord's Winchester was gone from its deer-antler rest over the stone fireplace. All the glasses and jars in the kitchen had been smashed.

"All right, you men!" Murray said harshly. "Take a good look! Remember!"

Sibley turned toward Carter and told him to fall out with a burial detail. They could find shovels in the stable, he said.

When the men began to dismount, Murray said, "Where the hell are you going?"

"To get shovels, sir," Carter said, surprised. "Going to bury—"

"Who the hell told you to do that?"

"I did, sir."

"Sibley, I give the orders around here. Prepare to mount! Mount!"

"Sir, the wolves—"

"Sibley, I'm warning you! The Colcord cowboys'll show up in a day or two. Let them do the work. Back to the road!"

From the far side of the *malpais*, Nachodise watched them. He was praying that the major would ride after them. He had a Winchester now as well as Slocum's Colt, and he was sure that he could kill the major easily at a hundred feet. He had a good horse he had taken from the Colcords' corral. It was with strong disappointment that he watched the column head back to the road. He had seen the patrol coming out of the fort, and he had deliberately flourished his trail, hoping that they would follow. He hoped that the major would get himself into a spot where he might be helpless even for a shot from Slocum's Colt. But it was not meant to happen today. Another day, he promised himself. I am patient.

He signaled the rest of the war party to continue. He had led them to a good day's work. They knew that he had good medicine. In the future, he would have no opposition when he suggested another raid. There were some very good men on the reservation who were having strong second thoughts about remaining peaceful. It would be easy now to recruit them. The wiping out of Nachodise's little band and other Murray attacks were making all the Apaches angry and restless.

\* \* \*

Sibley had been placed in command of the scouts because of his ability to speak Spanish, his general common sense, and his grasp of the geography of the country as well as his feel for the psychology of the Indian. Now he was riding beside them as they trotted back to the road.

"*Qué pasó arriba?*" he asked quietly. "What happened up there?"

They shrugged. The *comandante*, they said, had just sat on his horse up on the ridge. They could see the war party about a mile or a mile and a quarter away from the ranch house. It would have been easy to chase them away, the scout said, gallop after them, yell, fire a few shots. That would have given the Colcords time to see what was happening. They could have barred their door and gotten their guns ready. The Apaches wouldn't stand still for three well-armed soldiers. They would utter a few defiant yells and then race off. The scout said that he had waited for the *comandante* to give the obvious, necessary order. But instead, he only smiled and said that they would have to go back and get the rest of the soldiers.

"*Que tonto!*" the Pima finished. "How stupid!"

No, not stupid, Sibley thought. Crazy, maybe, but not stupid. He knows what he's doing, the son of a bitch! He turned in his saddle. Sure enough, Murray was riding in the middle of his bodyguard. His face wore a contented smile.

## 18

Slocum rested from his digging. He was sitting at the table where Murray and the man from Tucson would be sitting. Johansen was away somewhere on the post.

"Good morning, Mr. Bearclaw."

He rose. "Good mornin', ma'am."

"Ah!" she said, surprised. "I see that you have been well brought up. You have an accent, Mr. Bearclaw, a soft, pleasant one. If you were not a mountain man, I would have guessed that you came from Mississippi and had a tutor when a child."

She had hit both truths right on the head. Slocum forced a smile. "No, ma'am, I'm from Virginia. My father was a schoolteacher, and my mother insisted on us children havin' good manners."

"Oh." Her eyes were raking him. "We were stationed in Virginia a while," she said pleasantly.

"And later in Mississippi. I've always felt rather confident that I could tell the difference between the two accents. The Mississippi accent is much broader, more intense. The Virginia accent is far more soft, far more gentle. But no matter." She was holding a sketch pad in her hands. She put it on the counter.

But it did matter, Slocum thought. She was a very perceptive woman. She could be dangerous.

"They say that only a man who has killed a grizzly with a knife has the right to wear such a necklace."

"That's true. Excuse me, ma'am, I have to go and earn a livin'."

Johansen came in and said, "Morning, Mrs. Murray."

"Good morning, Mr. Johansen. I have no intention of keeping you from your work, Mr. Bearclaw. I'll just follow you outside and do some sketching. Mr. Johansen, I promise not to interfere with his work."

Johansen shrugged.

"And do, please, Mr. Bearclaw, wear that magnificent necklace."

Slocum did not like this at all. Whatever Major Murray was like, he certainly would not enjoy the idea of his wife sketching Slocum. He went into the storeroom and took the necklace from the crudely carpentered little table where he kept his odds and ends. He slid it over his head, walked out, and stepped into the hole. He took a plank, placed it across two sawhorses, measured the length he wanted, and began sawing.

She had followed him out, carrying a small kitchen chair. She sat on it and crossed her legs.

Placing the sketch pad on her lap, she said, "No, no. Without your shirt, please."

Slocum hesitated, but there was no way out of it. On the frontier men did not remove their shirts in front of respectable women.

"It's perfectly all right," she said, laughing. "I can supply a letter of reference from my husband. Now take off your shirt, please. The light is perfect."

She waited, tapping her charcoal pencil impatiently against the pad. Slocum took a deep breath and then removed his shirt. He resumed sawing while she began a fast charcoal sketch.

"Very good trapezoids," she said as she worked. "Your back seems to be well covered with scars."

"Horse threw me onto a roll of barbed wire."

"I understand you're making a joke," she said coldly. "Be so good as to remember that I've been an army wife for a long time. I know bullet wounds when I see them. I know knife wounds, bayonet wounds, and shrapnel wounds. I can tell them apart. I see a couple of bullet wounds in your back. Now, they come from being shot at by a coward—or from being shot at by people riding hard after you. And around these parts, that usually means a posse. What do you say to that, Mr. Bearclaw?"

Slocum's stomach churned within him. She was a very smart woman. She smiled at him and bent down to her sketching. He kept sawing. She held up her sketch.

"Very good, ma'am."

"You mean the sketch?"

"Yes, ma'am."

"And now for another pose. Do you mind lifting that sledgehammer?"

She folded over the sketch and waited with a

clean page. Slocum picked up the six-pound hammer and held it high in the air.

"A very poor pose, Mr. Bearclaw. Too stiff, too theatrical." She snapped the charcoal pencil in an irritated manner and stood up abruptly. Then she walked close to the edge of the pit and spoke very quietly: "Major Murray is leaving late this afternoon on one of his nasty little expeditions. He calls them 'defensive patrols.'" She laughed ironically. "I don't like what he's doing. I know what's happening on those patrols. I know a fine way to make my point clear. I hope you understand me."

Slocum was only too sure that he understood.

"This evening I might take a little stroll. I might walk down to the river. I might walk to it from the back of the officers' quarters. If the enlisted men want anything to do with the laundresses or the half-breed girls, they take them behind the enlisted mens' barracks. They never come on our side. And *none* of the officers' wives would be found dead along the river. Of course, they're such dull little frumps that no one would ever ask them to the river, anyway. And they're all dreadfully afraid of malicious gossip, which is always the best kind. In an army post like this, there are only two things to do, you see. The first is malicious gossip, for which I have no patience. And the second thing is to work for your husband's promotion. I've had no need to do that; he became a hero immediately. Eleven o'clock will be fine. And one more thing—I am serious about this—don't wash."

She closed the sketch pad, smiled, and walked away. As much as Slocum had reason to fear the damage she was capable of doing to his plans, he had to admit that her long legs and full breasts might overcome his natural reluctance to tangle with her. She obviously planned to use him to make her husband change his ways. It would not end well. That last request of hers was so baffling that Slocum gave up thinking about it.

He worked hard all afternoon, sawing and hammering in the full glare of the sun. He drank quarts of water, and it all went through him almost instantly, soaking his underdrawers as well as his pants and undershirt. He lifted an arm and smelled himself. God, he smelled pretty bad.

By six o'clock Slocum had floored the pit and nailed up the side panels. He made sure that the nails that held the panel in front of the entrance to his hidden tunnel were short and easily pulled out by a hard wrench at the bottom of the panel. He cut out window openings. The next day he would put the roof on.

Just before suppertime, Johansen took a sniff and said, "Aren't you going to wash? You smell like a horse."

"Tonight I'm going down to the river and take a swim."

"There's Apaches out there, Brian. Especially now that the major's got them riled up."

Slocum shrugged. "I'll take my chances," he said.

Johansen sighed. "Take my Colt along," he said. There was no more reference made to the river.

After supper, Johansen went out and looked at the shed. "Mighty nice work," he said, impressed. He came in and sat down at the table and sipped his coffee. "Did you hear reveille this morning?"

Slocum nodded.

"How'd it sound?"

"Ragged."

"Damn right! The trumpeter let someone who

168   JAKE LOGAN

wanted to practice sound it for fifty cents. Both are in the guardhouse, waiting for Murray. Did you ever see such chicken-feed rules? Only in the army, my friend. Only in the army. You look awful tired. Going to bed early?"

"I am. I need rest."

Slocum lay down on his cot in the storeroom. He was exhausted, but he dare not fall asleep. If he didn't show up at eleven, there was no telling what that uninhibited and clearly vindictive woman might do. She could ask the federal marshal to drop in and look him over; she could ask General Sherman at the Department of the West's headquarters in Omaha to see whether anyone of Slocum's description might be an army deserter. Slocum suddenly sat bolt upright when he realized that she might have had an ulterior motive in making those drawings of him. She could send one to the marshal and one to Omaha, with a notation on the back describing all the scars on his torso. Omaha might have some veteran officer in the provost marshal's office who just might be reminded of a certain John Slocum, late of the Confederate Army, who in May 1865 shot and killed a Northern cavalry captain. The cavalry took care of its own.

But he would just have to get along with her until his work was done at the fort. He didn't know how long that would take. A minimum of a month, perhaps. This job gave off that month-long smell. He had done enough of them to get the feel. Until then he would just have to sit up and bark whenever she snapped her fingers. He could see no way out of it, no way at all.

At five minutes to eleven, Johansen's noisy alarm clock rattled at his table. Slocum shut it off before it would wake Johansen. He pulled on his boots, shoved the Colt into his belt, and walked along the back of the enlisted men's quarters, where he disturbed two giggling couples. Then he cut across the parade ground and walked around the officers' quarters with their yellow light spilling from the windows. He walked for two hundred yards to the grove of cottonwoods that grew beside the river. Under his feet the dead leaves and twigs snapped and rustled. The night wind was cool. He sat with his back against a tree, watching the brown river slide smoothly by.

"You come on time," a voice said.

Slocum jumped. She had been sitting on the other side of the tree.

"I even knew which tree you'd pick out."

God damn it! Slocum thought.

She leaned on the tree. "Come around to this side," she ordered. He obeyed. She had cleared the ground of its leaves and twigs and had spread a Navajo blanket. She took a deep breath. "Good!" she said. "I like to be under cottonwoods with all those little dried leaves and bits of branches on the ground. Then no one can creep up on us. Don't you agree?"

"Yes," Slocum answered. His throat was suddenly dry. He hadn't slept with a woman since that aborted attempt with Dilchay. Was it two or three months ago? And before that, before the failed bank robbery, it had been two months. One woman in five months! No wonder he was excited.

She patted the blanket. Slocum sat down.

"I am going to tell you something that not even my husband knows." She put a hand on his knee. "When I was thirteen, I was walking home one day from school." Her hand began to move upward on his thigh, gently kneading. "It was early spring in Michigan. They were cutting timber far up a river which flowed by our town. There were always lumberjacks; they came into town to get drunk and find a woman."

The tips of her fingers were just brushing against the length of Slocum's penis. It began to swell.

"Since the wild flowers were blooming in the woods, I always went home by a shortcut so I could pick violets. One of them was sleeping off a drunk in a clump of bushes. I thought he was dead. I ducked under and shook him. He woke up. I was well developed for my age. He was still drunk, I suppose. No one was around. He tore off my underclothes and raped me. I was a virgin. He held his hand over my mouth. No one would have heard my screams, anyway; it was too far from the road. Then he ran away into the woods. I never saw him again, but I measure all men against him."

Her hand was gently brushing along the length of Slocum's penis.

"He gave me my first orgasm. I don't think I have ever had one of such intensity in all my married life. Oh, God, I was so excited! And he hadn't taken a bath all winter, the way those lumberjacks do. They wait till spring." Her hand was now gripping Slocum's penis feverishly.

"I want you to rip my clothes off and rape me." She spoke quickly, her breath coming in hot little gusts.

Slocum stared at her. He took no pleasure in rape. He had never done it; in fact, he had shot one of his gang for that crime.

"Don't worry," she said, not understanding his expression. "This is an old dress. I brought another along to go home in. No one saw me come out.

And if they did, in the darkness they didn't know the color of it, anyway." She jerked her head. Suspended from a branch of a nearby cottonwood was a dress.

Slocum smiled at the blend of careful planning and passion.

She slapped him suddenly as hard as she could. "Don't you laugh at me, you son of a bitch!" she hissed.

People did not say that to Slocum and get away with it. His reflexes were fast. As soon as her palm left his face, he grabbed it and jerked. The movement pulled her in close. He had never struck a woman, but now he was tempted.

Her breasts, free of the corset, brushed against Slocum's shirt. Without warning she spat in his face and punched him hard in the kidneys with sharp little knuckles. It hurt. In a sudden wave of rage, he tore her dress open, exposing her naked torso from the shoulders to the waist. In the darkness under the interwoven branches of the trees, her flesh shone like ivory. Her nipples were dark.

"Yes!" She gasped.

She took his left hand and bit it as hard as she could. It was a serious bite. Slocum knew how to deal with biters. He pinched her nose until she opened her mouth. A concentric ring of tooth marks curved across his palm. In spite of his anger, he knew what she was doing. She wanted to infuriate him so that he would, in reality, rape her. Well, by God, he thought angrily, if that's what she wants she can have it! He ripped the rest of her dress apart. The effort pulled her around like a rag doll, and she moaned with excitement.

Underneath the dress, she was naked except for her midthigh black stockings tied on with garters and black ankle-top buttoned shoes. Her hands tore frantically at Slocum's shirt. She unbuttoned it, her hands trembling violently. When it was pulled from Slocum's shoulders, he kicked off his boots. Her wildly shaking hands plunged into his fly and pulled out his penis. She fell to her knees and rammed his penis as deep into her throat as she could.

Moaning, she slid her wet, hot mouth up and down Slocum's penis while she cupped his balls in her hands. Before he came to a climax, he pushed her away, in spite of her whimper of dismay. Paying no attention, he pushed her hard. She fell on her back onto the ground, with a moan of excitement. He pulled her legs wide apart and kneeled between them. She grabbed his penis and inserted it into her dripping wet vagina. He seized a wrist in each hand and pinned them above her head. Then he rammed his penis in as hard as he could.

"Yes!" she screamed. "Yes!"

She strained her head around and buried her nose in his armpit. Slocum knew that with a day's sweat on his body, he must be smelling ripe, but she inhaled deeply and groaned. She dug her nails into his back. Slocum did not go for that kind of behavior in lovemaking, but this woman so angered him that he held her throat with one hand while he pumped ever deeper into her with each violent thrust. He drove her backward across the tree litter for a yard, and then her wild, amazing orgasm came and shook her the way a dog shakes a rat.

"Oh, my God!" she moaned. "Oh, oh, oh!"

Slocum felt her cunt squeezing his penis. It kept squeezing and relaxing as if it were her hand. She pounded her heels on his back in ecstasy, shook all over with an orgasm that was not so strong as the first, and then gave a long, shuddering half moan, half gasp. Then she suddenly went limp.

*Jesus!* he thought. She lay there for a minute. Then she brusquely shoved him off as if he were a big dog that had pressed itself against her when she was not in the mood to throw any more sticks for him to chase. He lay beside her, panting, until his breathing resumed its normal pace.

She sat up. Her back was covered with dirt and dried leaves. She reached out, picked up her torn dress, bunched it up, and handed it to him. She jerked her head. Slocum understood the gesture. He rubbed her back clean.

"Clean?" she asked briskly.

"Yes, ma'am."

"I like the way you make love. I know you will be very discreet about mentioning this to anyone."

Slocum said nothing.

"To start with, my husband would kill you."

Slocum thought: If only she knew that my aim in being at the fort is to do just the opposite!

She stood up and reached for the dress that was hanging from a branch. She slid it on as if the cottonwood grove were her bedroom in her own home.

"I said something to you," she said coldly. "I would like an answer." She reached into a pocket of her dress, pulled out a few hairpins, and held some in her teeth. One by one she inserted them. Slocum sat up and watched her with his arms folded. She was one slick article, he thought.

She finished, patted her hair into place, and said, "Well?" Her voice was not friendly, Slocum decided.

"Sure."

"Sure *what*?"

There was a vicious tone to the last word that Slocum did not like. She was like a very unhappy spinster schoolteacher he once had, before his father decided that a male tutor would be a better choice for a growing and vigorous boy. It was as if her bitterness could somehow be softened or made more bearable by her being mean to him.

"Nobody'll know."

"That's what I wanted to hear you say." She bent down and picked up the torn dress. She began to fold it carefully. "Thank you, then. I've enjoyed our talk. You needn't escort me back, thank you." Now she was as prim as a young girl on her first date. She stood, holding her folded dress. "The night is getting quite chilly, isn't it?"

"It certainly is, ma'am." If she wanted to pretend that all they had done was have a casual chat, Slocum was willing.

"Tomorrow, however, will be hot."

"I suspect so, Mrs. Murray." He kept his voice deferential.

If that was what she wanted, she was going to get it. She was as dangerous to him as a coiled, angry diamondback. He did not want to do anything that might make her strike, but he did appreciate one thing: She had let him know how dangerous she could be. She turned abruptly and walked away.

Slocum stared at the sinuous sway of her ass under the tight white dress. Gradually it disappeared under the shadows of the trees; for a while he heard the twigs snapping under her feet. When there was silence in the grove, he pulled out a lump of soap from his pants pocket. He stepped in the river and scrubbed himself thoroughly. The soap stung his back where she had scratched it.

Tomorrow he would ask Johansen to smear some iodine on it. Thank God, he thought, he wouldn't have to be there long. He'd wind up giving her a few hard slaps to teach her a lesson about manners, but she would probably love it and ask for more. Or she might ask Omaha to check him out and see what his real name was.

Tuesday would see the whole thing settled one way or the other. That intimate talk Murray had demanded might be the key to everything.

Slocum wiped himself dry with his flannel shirt, slid on his pants and boots, stuck the Colt in his belt, and draped the shirt over his shoulders. He began to walk back. It had grown chilly. Far off, on the edge of the hills, a coyote was talking to another one. The friend was somewhere near his grove. Slocum liked coyotes for their curiosity about everything and their cheerful insolence. He listened with a smile on his face.

Suddenly he remembered that Apaches signaled at night with coyote calls. He froze. Very slowly he dropped to his knees and then flat on his belly. He was removing the free gift of his profile from any possible enemy. Before he went prone, he very carefully felt the ground where he would be lying. He removed every dried leaf and twig. When he was at last stretched out flat with the Colt in his hand, he was as silent as a moth. He cupped his free hand behind his left ear and waited for the sound of someone approaching. The coyote had entered the grove. It made the announcement loudly to its distant friend.

The problem for Slocum was this: Would an Apache nearing a possible white victim proclaim his existence so obviously? No, he would not. On the other hand, Slocum reasoned, if the victim were to hear some noise on the dry floor of a cottonwood grove, he might very well assume that it was being made by a coyote looking for a careless squirrel as it frisked from tree to tree.

So it was six of one and a half a dozen of the other. Best to be vigilant. There came suddenly the faintest sound of a leaf being pressed flat and then cracking under pressure. The noise seemed to be about fifty feet in front of him. Then there was silence. Slocum didn't want to pull back the hammer of the Colt. The *click* would signal precisely where he was. A sudden dive onto him with a knife would be the inevitable result. It was not easy to plan a defense against a knife attack if you did not know where the attack would be coming from.

The rim of the rising moon slid over the surrounding ridge. The grove lit up as if a row of footlights had been turned on. Very slowly, Slocum moved his left palm so that it covered the barrel of the Colt. A random bit of moonlight might hit it and silently announce his presence to the man who might be circling him slowly and with infinite care.

A wind sprang up. Slocum took a long, deep breath. Sometimes a man could smell an Indian's sweat, especially if the Indian had been traveling where water was scarce and had been out all day in the hot sun. The wind did not bring any odor of sweat. But then again, Slocum thought, maybe the Indian had found a creek or a waterfall in the mountains. He could have washed.

A very faint crackling noise came from his right. Slocum judged the distance to be thirty feet, no more. Very slowly he turned his head and shoulders until they were straining in that direction. It was too soon to pull back the hammer; that would have to wait till the final charge. Slocum felt his heart beating faster, until he was sure that the sound had to be audible to anyone within several feet. But he knew it was only an illusion.

A twig snapped thirty feet to the rear. Whoever it was, he was very carefully and very methodically circling Slocum. He suddenly realized that he had not heard the other coyote for some time. Maybe it was beginning its approach from another angle as part of a prearranged plan. That was clever, Slocum thought. A simultaneous attack, launched from two directions. They were counting upon a momentary indecision as to what side he would respond to first—and then it would be too late. He felt sweat break out on his face.

Ten feet to the rear a twig snapped. Close enough! Slocum fell onto his belly and pulled back the hammer.

He faced a startled half-grown coyote. At his unexpected move, the coyote recoiled and sat back on his haunches with an amazed expression. Then he stood up and began to wag his tail. His mouth opened in a grin. He bent his front legs, barked with excitement, danced sideward, and barked once more. Opening his jaws, he let his tongue loll out.

"I'll be a son of a bitch!" Slocum said aloud. "The little bastard wants to play!"

He had picked up Slocum's scent, circled him warily, and then decided that the strange animal, although it had four legs, was for some strange reason lying on its belly. It might be lured into a game of some kind. At the sound of Slocum's voice, the coyote barked again. Slocum let down the hammer carefully.

The other coyote barked in an annoyed, peremptory fashion. The pup's ears pricked in that direction. Slocum stood up and shoved the Colt into his belt. The coyote looked at him with renewed interest and expectation. The other coyote barked once more.

"Go home to your mother before you catch hell, kid," Slocum said.

All the way back to the storeroom, he kept laughing. Later he realized that it was the first time he had laughed with real pleasure for months. He knew that he would cherish this funny, warm memory in the weeks ahead.

There would be nothing else funny ahead for him at all.

## 19

Johansen drenched a tuft of sterile cotton with iodine and swabbed it over the scratches on Slocum's back. Slocum winced.

"Don't complain," Johansen told him. "You enjoyed getting them, I bet you. And I tell you something, Brother Bearclaw, it wasn't a squaw, either."

"What makes you think so?"

"Simple. Squaws work hard all the time. Their nails are short. Whoever did this doesn't spend her time over a washboard. That means it's not a Mex gal, either. I have a feeling it's one of the officers' wives."

He threw the swab away and then happened to catch sight of Slocum's face. It was not an expression that could be described as friendly.

"On the other hand," Johansen went on, "you might've borrowed Dolly and went for a ride to

Tucson. She stepped on a piece of baling wire, thought it was a rattlesnake, and bucked you clear through the window of Campbell's drug store. That's much more likely, isn't it?"

"That's just what happened."

"I figured. Now, think we'll get it roofed over today?"

"Sure. And this afternoon we can move in all the tables and shelves."

"Fine, fine." Johansen chuckled with pleasure. He stood and pulled a notebook from under the counter. "Then tomorrow I'll start working on the formula."

"The one for smokeless powder?"

"You've got a good memory! Yep, that one. I'm sure I'm close to it. And if I find it, I'm going to make you a proposition."

Slocum got the tools from the storeroom and carried them out back. He returned and picked up a stack of one by sixes.

"Aren't you curious?" Johansen asked.

"Sure I'm curious. But you'll tell me when you're ready."

Johansen chuckled again. "I guess that's why I like you, Bearclaw. You talk just enough and not a word more. So here's the deal: If I develop this smokeless powder, the first thing I have to do is go to Washington with a few pounds of it and demonstrate it to those lubberheads in the War Department. Writing letters back and forth can take years."

"Taking a few pounds along?"

"Yep."

"Explode it on the lawn?"

"Something like that." He looked at Slocum. "All right. Spit it out. What's on your mind?"

"That won't impress them much."

"Why not?" Johansen started to bristle.

"How will they know that the powder will push a bullet?"

Johansen slapped the table. "By God, you're right! You're saying I ought to load a box of Springfield .45-70 cartridges here and take them with me. Shoot them off at a target down at the arsenal, eh? By God, I like that idea. Soon's I work out the formula, I'll load the cartridges. Fifty'll be enough. I'll take a day for that. Then I'll take the next army ambulance up to the train at Benson. Wait a day or two for the train. A week later, I'll be in Washington. A week, two weeks at the most, then I'll get to see my generals. A week more, and I'll be back here. So, Bearclaw, you want to run the store till I come back? I'll pay you well. How about it?"

Slocum hated to agree. If he found his chance and killed the major, he certainly wasn't going to hang around the fort and take care of the store. On the other hand, if he said no to Johansen's offer, Johansen might not be so friendly; he'd look for someone else to run it. If that happened, he wouldn't need Slocum around any more, particularly since the laboratory would be finished today. Slocum knew that he wanted to stay at the fort for two reasons. He had to listen Tuesday night to Major Murray's talk. Also, he was beginning to get a very good idea of how to kill the major, even though Murray would be surrounded by his efficient, tough escort. For the problem was not only to kill the major but to get away safely.

With Johansen's unwitting help, Slocum had just realized how he might solve that problem. Slocum would have to lie. He did so with regret, for he admired and liked Johansen.

"I'd be pleased, real pleased."

"Well, that's fine, just fine, Brother Bearclaw!" Johansen said happily, slapping him on the shoulder. "My worries are over!"

Slocum felt worse than ever. He went out and got rid of his tension by laboring furiously all afternoon. By evening all the bottles, retorts, porcelain mortars and pestles, glass beakers, and big glass jars full of sulphur, charcoal, saltpeter, and substances whose names meant nothing to Slocum were neatly lined up on shelves below ground level. If an accidental explosion happened, the gases would be safely vented upward.

When Slocum had finally finished, he rested with a mug of hot coffee that Johansen had brought out to him. Major Murray suddenly appeared at the shed door and looked inside.

"Looks safe enough, Johansen. Going to go on with your experiments?"

Slocum put the cup down and began unpacking test tubes.

"Yes, Major."

"Don't look at me for help in Washington," Murray said sourly. "They'd like to wrap my guts around a stepladder."

"Yes, sir."

"I hope your plan works out, Johansen. I'm losing too many men with this damn black powder. Apaches see it, and if they're close enough with their arrows, there's an end to a good man. With this smokeless we can do a lot more damage and kill a lot more of the bastards."

As Slocum placed the test tubes in their racks, he felt a surge of hatred. He felt Murray's eyes upon him, and so he kept his face impassive. He bent down and took out more tubes from their sawdust packing. As he straightened up, he caught the major's eye.

"Lots of people don't like me," the major said. "Especially lately."

The ever-present six-man bodyguard had surrounded the store, bored but vigilant. Slocum felt sure that Murray had told them that if they ever slipped up, he would fry their balls in olive oil or something equally unsettling. He hoped that Mrs. Murray hadn't told her husband about her trip down to the cottonwood grove. He didn't think that she had, but God only knew what an angry woman might say to get revenge.

"For instance, do you like me?" he heard the major say.

Slocum thought for a second that the major was talking to Johansen, but when the question was repeated, he realized with a chilling sensation in the pit of his stomach that it was meant for him. Johansen was silent. Slocum turned. Murray had pulled off his buckskin riding gloves and was slapping them idly against his blue trousers.

"Well?" Murray asked again. There was a tone of irritation in the question.

Slocum thought how much he disliked both the Murrays. If he were to anger the male side of the family, he could be ruled off the fort immediately, since he was only a civilian employed there at the commanding officer's pleasure.

"Got no reason to like or dislike you," Slocum said politely.

"Good! An honest answer." The major slapped his gloves hard against the trousers. "You did this carpentry work?"

"Yes, sir."

"You're good at it. I might need you to put up a

few shelves in my house. Mrs. Murray's been after me. All the men in my command are all thumbs."

"Sure."

"Just keep out of trouble and don't bring in any liquor to the fort, and I think we can do business. Johansen's last helper got run off that way, eh?" He turned to Johansen. "All right, Johansen, I'll be in tonight at seven. You'll take care of everything the usual way? Goat's milk?"

"Yes, Major. Everything will be ready."

"Good."

At six-thirty, Slocum stood up and took his last sip of coffee. He went into the storeroom and picked up a blanket.

"Off to sleep out there?" Johansen asked as he unhooked a jar of goat's milk that had been suspended from the porch rail.

"Yep."

"Wouldn't you rather have a girl in that blanket instead of a friendly rattler?"

Slocum remarked that it was hard to tell the difference sometimes. Johansen took off the wet burlap he had wrapped around the clay jar of goat's milk. Evaporation in the warm wind had cooled the jar nicely. He set it on the table and began to fill the kerosene lantern.

"See you in the morning, then."

"Good night," Slocum answered.

He walked outside the store and around to the rear. No one was in sight. He quickly ducked into the laboratory. It didn't matter whether anyone had seen him go in. No one would be suspicious. A man who had been working all week on a structure went in and out so often that he would never be noticed.

## SLOCUM AND THE MAD MAJOR 185

Once inside, Slocum crawled under the table he had set against the far wall. He slid the panel sideward on its upper and lower grooves. The tunnel was now exposed. He took a bottle of water he had set inside during the afternoon. He folded his blanket and tossed it inside the tunnel. He crawled in, slid the panel back into position, and worked his way on his hands and knees to the tunnel's end. Reaching upward, he brushed his hand back and forth until he felt the bottom end of the soaped dowel. Satisfied, he lay down on the blanket and placed the water jar by his head. The heat was thick and clammy, and his shirt was already drenched. He waited.

Slocum could hear Johansen walking back and forth over his head. He heard the sound of glasses being set down. Johansen was humming, probably because of his feeling that the long, drawn-out experiments with his smokeless powder looked as if they were coming to a successful conclusion.

Slocum heard heavy steps drumming across the front porch. There was more than one man. It had to be Murray and his bodyguard. Then someone clattered down the four wooden steps into the laboratory, hawked, spat on the floor, then clattered back up the steps. More steps came across the floor. Voices rumbled. It was impossible to understand what was being said. That would have to wait until he could withdraw the dowel. Various steps sounded across the floor and then across the porch. The bodyguard was surrounding the building. Slocum heard nervous steps going back and forth. That would be Murray, alone. The steps moved to the porch.

He heard Murray call out loudly, "Anyone in sight?"

Then he heard someone call out, "Buggy's comin' down the road with an escort."

Now was the time. Murray was out of the room, and no one else was there. Slocum reached up and twisted the dowel. It broke free easily, and he pulled it down. Cool air flowed down onto his soaking face. A round yellow column of light streamed down into the tunnel.

He heard Murray say, "Good. Bring him in as soon as he gets here. Unhitch the horses and give them a feed."

Murray paced back and forth. Within a minute, a team pulled up outside. Horses snorted. Slocum could hear the creaking of saddle leather as several men dismounted. Footsteps sounded across the porch.

Murray said, "On time."

"I'm always on time," a voice said gently. "Is that my milk?"

"Yes," Murray answered with barely concealed disgust.

"Thank you."

Slocum lay backward with his arms under his head. His ear was turned to the hole. He heard Bailey taking a long sip.

"Ah," Bailey said. He took another sip. "It's been a long, dusty ride. And I can tell you, I was a bit nervous. All those Apaches. I can hear a little sloshing sound from the metal hip flask you're wearing. You may as well take a drink."

"Don't you patronize me," Murray said. His voice was thick with suppressed rage. "I wanted to talk to you. I've done plenty for you, and don't you forget it!"

"Lower your voice, please."

"Don't you—" Murray began, but he subsided as

he realized that his voice would probably carry to the two men stationed on the porch outside. He abruptly stood up, reached the door in two fast steps, and jerked it open. One man was standing there, leaning against a porch pillar with an arm outstretched at full length, holding a Winchester with its butt on the porch. The muzzle was in his hand. Another man was walking slowly back and forth, alternately meeting the guards who were patrolling along the sides. Satisfied that no one was eavesdropping, Murray grunted and closed the door. He walked back and took his chair again.

When he spoke it was with a lower tone: "I've been running these aggressive patrols for three months, Bailey. Did it work out as we planned?"

"Major—"

"Let me finish! *I* called for this meeting, not you. I'll tell you exactly what happened. I provoked at least twenty peaceful bands out their safe hideyholes in the Santa Cruz and in the Superstitions. They were living far from any white settlement or ranch. That was the scheme, right? Well, answer me, damn it!"

"Yes, Major. It was part of the scheme."

"Then, according to plan, they hit the warpath. Right?"

"Right."

"They burned stagecoaches. They ambushed wagon trains. They burned ranch houses. And they burned a lot of people, too. Am I right?"

"Alas."

"Alas, he says. And then Chato's people left the reservation up in San Carlos and started in, too. That was foreseen and part of the plan. And then what happened?" Murray took two long deep and angry breaths and said, louder, "What happened, God damn it?"

"The army lost forty dead. Civilian dead, as far as is known, is a hundred and thirty."

"Yes, yes, I know that," Murray said impatiently. "And what else?"

"The Mexican government asked us to slow down. Too many of the Chiricahuas were being forced over the border, and they were stirring up trouble down there."

"To hell with the goddamn greasers! Since you're so shy, I'm going to tell you. And then I'm going to tell you why I'm mad. And then I'm going to tell you what you're going to do about it. Washington sent eight more companies to the department here. That's a lot of men and a lot of horses. Men eat beans and meat and drink coffee, and horses eat a lot of hay. Who owns the wholesale houses in Tucson? Who owns a lot of nearby ranches with the beef?"

"I do."

"And who cut his hay last year and held it for such a fine time to sell to the quartermaster?"

"It's time to stop this childish game, Murray."

"*Game* is it? And who, following our plan, ordered the quartermaster to buy the beef, the beans, the horses, the mules, and the hay from you? Who ordered the quartermaster to rent your wagons to carry the stuff in? *Who?*"

It had all suddenly become clear to Slocum: the unprovoked raids, the constant, senseless harrying of the Apaches, the murder of their women and children. Waves of furious rage swept over him. He put the end of the dowel in his mouth and bit it in order to channel the energy that threatened to force him out of the tunnel, wrest a Winchester from a guard, and kill Murray or Bailey. He slowly became aware, as through a red cloud, of Murray's continuing complaints.

"I totaled the quartermaster vouchers, Bailey. You took in close to $450,000 up to last month. You must have cleared a quarter of a million at least! And you wouldn't have made more than a twentieth of that if I hadn't gone along with your great idea. No, let me finish! When are you going to keep your share of the bargain?"

"Murray—"

"Answer me, God damn it! I have an angry wife to handle. She's going crazy out here in this godforsaken post! I promised her she'd be out of here two months ago. You keep your promises, or by God—"

"Or what?" Bailey asked calmly. "You'll tell the newspapers that you deliberately tried to incite the Apaches to burn up this part of Arizona so that you could make money for me? So that you could be called a hero? And then tell them that our deal was that I'd see you become the territorial governor? And that you have a dream to become President? Think it over, Murray. Think it over calmly. Take your time."

Slocum thought, So this is the man who controls the political life of Arizona. This piece of scum, this shit. At least when I rob a bank, I make no hypocritical statements about my service. He's even worse than Murray.

Murray had said nothing for several seconds.

"Very good," Bailey told him. "You've thought it over. Now, I've made this trip because you said it was very important for you to speak to me face to face. Fine; I came, I listened. Now you will listen to me. It takes a lot of time to talk to the people who run each county here. It takes time to persuade them to agree with me that you'd be the perfect man for the next governor. I have to do a lot of arm twisting. I have to call in a lot of favors. I have to deal with a lot of committees in the Senate in Washington. I have to write to the majority leader in the Senate. I have to talk to the editors of all the newspapers in Arizona. I have to promise them I'll take out a lot of ads for my grain and beef and haulin' outfits. I have to pay out a bribe here and a bribe there. I have to talk to editors at a few influential papers in Washington.

"And when it all comes together—and it *will*, in a month or two—we can begin to bang the drum for you. And I tell you right now that a couple of daring, risky victories over a nice, big, vicious war party that's killed a lot of people will be the perfect kind of food to give the editors. They'd like that. I'd like that. They could write big long editorials about your bravery and your grasp of military strategy. They'd write that you're repeating your brilliant Civil War record, but this time you're doing it with a cruel and savage enemy. I know that's what the editors would like to write, because I've already paid Anderson for such an editorial—he's up in Flagstaff—and I've paid Emerson in Tucson for the same kind of writing. That's $2,000 I've already paid out.

"And when they write that editorial, they've agreed to write that a man of such administrative abilities would be a perfect choice for governor once you've gone and wiped out the red murderers."

"I see." Murray's voice was quiet and thoughtful.

"And that's what I've been doing all this time. Got any more goat's milk?"

Slocum heard Murray get up and walk around, obviously looking for more milk.

"I guess that's all there is."

"A shame. It was nice and cool. Are there any more questions? No? I'm sorry you're having trouble with your wife. A beautiful woman. Does she have any idea of what you're doing?"

"Of course not!"

"You *might* have told her. A nagging woman can drive a man mad. Remember what Shakespeare said. A nagging woman is worse than a leaking roof or a smoky chimney."

"No," Murray said. "I don't remember what Shakespeare said. I was busy fighting a war."

"Yes. Well, I have to go. This will be our last meeting until you're the new governor. It won't do for people to get the idea that we are meeting. If you have anything to ask, I'll send Gompertz."

"My wife detests him."

"My wife also. But he does as he's told. He is also incorruptible. Good evening."

Slocum heard the chairs being pushed back. Footsteps crossed the floor. Voices snapped orders. Bailey's ambulance pulled up. He heard the creaking of leather as the escort mounted and then the shaking of the harness. Then the ambulance rattled away.

Slocum lay in the tunnel a long time, thinking hard.

## 20

Upstairs in the storeroom, Slocum lay awake thinking the rest of the night. He wanted to kill both of them. Murray was the bigger problem; it would be just about impossible to get at him with his ever-present, ever-vigilant bodyguard. If Slocum didn't mind dying, he could get in a deadly shot before he would be wiped out very efficiently. He had seen the bodyguard at target practice behind the parade ground. Each man was a superb marksman.

The word "marksman" suddenly loomed up large in Slocum's mind. He, too, was a superb marksman. He should capitalize on that skill. The only way to do that would to shoot at such a distance that the bodyguard would be helpless to retaliate.

The question now became, Where was the place that would provide the distance? And what were the requirements? He would need a clear field of fire. There could be nothing that might deflect the bullet's flight. It had to be at a place where return fire would be ineffective. And the target would have to be motionless or moving slowly.

The only place it might work was Brown's Canyon, the narrow arroyo a couple miles south of the fort. It was a natural place for an ambush. Therefore, Slocum knew, it would be sensible for Murray's bodyguard to halt just before the canyon while they sent a man through to scout the lay of the land.

If Murray halted there, he would become a stationary target.

At the top of the slope overlooking the entrance to the canyon was a line of pine trees. Just behind the ridge, a man could keep a good horse saddled and ready, with a couple of saddlebags and some food. A good Arabian, such as the major's horse, for instance. The range would be over eight hundred yards. If a man had a long-barreled rifle like the Springfield, he might hit the major. He would need a massive bullet that would do serious damage, most likely fatal. That bullet the Springfield certainly had, with its 500-grain .45-caliber slug.

But the muzzle velocity wouldn't be enough—not at that distance, not downhill. If he only had a cartridge with a big bullet *and* with high muzzle velocity, he might just be able to do it.

Slocum sat bolt upright. Johansen had said that he was on the verge of developing smokeless powder! That would certainly help solve the concealment problem after the shot, and it would help give him a good head start before the bodyguard could figure out where the shot had come from.

As for the higher muzzle velocity, that would require a new mixture of chemicals. It required experimentation. It required a skillful chemist. And,

Slocum thought, he lived in the same house with one. Things might just work out if handled correctly. Slocum finally fell asleep.

"Now, I can finish up on the smokeless!" Johansen said. He was exultant. "I just want to shoot this batch."

The two men were walking to the firing range. Johansen held out his hand. In the palm four massive cartridges nestled. "They're loaded with my secret blend," he said. He looked at them affectionately. "Deadly little asparagus stalks, aren't they? Now, Brian, I want you to fire them at the target. I'm going off a bit and watch. I want you to get behind that little ridge over there and fire at the target. Keep moving around after each shot. Fire each cartridge from a different position. I don't want to see you. I want to see if I can spot the smoke."

"Right."

"You'll see I scratched a number on each casing: one, two, three, four, five. You see them?"

Slocum nodded.

"Purpose is to know which cartridge produces the least smoke. I varied the composition when I mixed them."

"Understood."

"All right. I'll walk a couple hundred yards across the range. When I turn around, drop flat and start shooting. In the correct sequence, mind."

Slocum waited till Johansen's slender body turned around and waved. He dropped flat, lined up the bull's-eye, and squeezed the trigger. He hadn't fired a gun in months. He preferred the Winchester to the Springfield because it was a better horse gun. The Springfield's steel barrel alone measured thirty inches. The gun weighed nine pounds, and only a man with strong chest and shoulder muscles could hold it steady enough to lock onto a target with any chance of success. To hold it on a man who was moving or sitting a nervous horse—and Murray's Arabian mare was certainly far removed from a placid plow horse—was well-nigh impossible. An absolutely solid rest was needed.

The Springfield bellowed like an angry bull. A hole one inch in diameter suddenly appeared on the lower right of the center ring of the bull's-eye. Not bad. He took the cartridge marked two and lifted the latch. Then he dropped in the long, thick cartridge, flipped the latch shut, and fired. Another hole appeared, just touching the first one. The next three shots all touched one another. Not bad at all, Slocum thought. He hadn't lost his touch, but it still wasn't good enough for the murderous accuracy needed to kill a man. More practice was required. He opened the latch, and the last shell jumped out. He stood up and walked around, picking up the empties. He was just in time to hand them to an ebullient, excited Johansen.

"Four and five! Four and five did it! They had no smoke, no smoke at all! I solved it, I solved it!" He danced with glee as he put the shells in his pocket. "Now I'll make up a batch of the four and five formulas to see which is the best. Then I'm off for Washington and fame and fortune!" He clapped Slocum on the back in his joy.

Slocum smiled at Johansen's pleasure. He swung the barrel of the rifle over his shoulder. On the parade ground, new recruits were being drilled in dismounting and firing quickly from a prone position. As Slocum and Johansen walked back, Slocum looked at Sibley. The captain was watching the recruits with a faintly disgusted look. A cigar stuck out of the corner of his mouth. Slocum was struck by Sibley's strong resemblance to Grant. He wondered what Sibley made of Murray's patrols. With Sibley in command, Slocum felt sure, there would be none of Murray's pitiless, aggressive attacks.

Slocum now began to test whether he could get Johansen to supply his ammunition wants. "I spent a lot of time up there," he began casually. He jerked his thumb at the distant ranges. "I figured I'd like to go back again, with a Springfield this time."

"It's a mighty heavy gun. Heavy to carry, too heavy for snap shooting, and the bullets tear too big a hole in the pelts. Winchester is a better deal. At least," he added, "seeing that I'm neither a hunter nor a trapper, that's what they all tell me."

A squad of cavalry trotted past. Two men wore only one spur each.

Johansen said, "See that? That's one way you can tell the major's not here. He'd eat those two men alive for breakfast, without salt. Sibley's more easygoing. He doesn't give a damn about spit and polish. Not like that crazy major, who wants the whole damned command here ready as if he were going to lead it down Pennsylvania Avenue!"

"The reason why I want the Springfield," Slocum said patiently, "is that I saw plenty of bighorn mountain sheep way up. Way, way up. There's no way I can ever get close to a mountain sheep."

"That's true."

"With a Winchester, that is."

"I think I can see what you're driving at, my boy."

"Yes. A Springfield's got a mighty long range. As

for ruinin' a pelt, hell, no one cares about that. All they want to nail up above the fireplace are the ram's horns."

"Damn right."

"And they'll pay plenty for good horns. I can spend a couple months up there, and I'll make plenty sellin' the horns to rich folks from the East."

"Right!"

"But what I need, Mr. Johansen, is a cartridge with enough powder to shove out that big slug with a high muzzle velocity."

"That's true. I think I see what you're after. You've solved the stalking problem with my smokeless powder. You might be able to plug a couple of rams. But the bullets won't reach across wide canyons or way up to a ridge or a peak. And you'll *never* be able to get close to a bighorn. You'd like me to see if I can pack in a higher explosive charge as well as making it smokeless. Am I right?"

Slocum smiled and nodded.

"Well, Brian, it's the least I can do for you. You've been mighty helpful to me in my old age. Come on down to my magnificent new laboratory."

Once down the steps, Johansen placed the empty casings on the table. He placed three glass jars on the table. The chemical names on each jar meant nothing to Slocum. Johansen carefully set a jeweler's delicate scales beside the jars.

"I have to be very, very accurate," he explained. "A grain too much of this potassium chlorate, and I might have too uncontrolled an explosion. Gunpowder burns at a predictable rate. That makes it safe to use. This stuff, I don't know. An instantaneous explosion would be disastrous. Maybe something between the two?"

He paused a moment and then weighed out

three small piles. He ground each pile down to a powder in the porcelain mortar.

"The smaller you make the surfaces, the faster the ignition," he explained. "The faster the ignition, the larger the volume of gas. The bigger the volume, the harder it pushes at the bullet. The harder it pushes, the faster the bullet goes. The faster it goes, the better your chances of bagging an animal with extraordinary vision, such as a bighorn."

He carefully poured the blend through a small funnel into the empty casing. He put in a primer and then reached for a steel-jacketed bullet.

"No," Slocum said.

"No what?"

"I want a lead bullet."

A lead bullet would expand on impact to twice its original diameter. Then it would push its mass through bone and muscle. The impact of such a monstrous projectile would knock any animal flat, and that went for any size up to a full-grown grizzly.

"Of course," Johansen said. "You'd need a bullet like that to knock a mountain sheep down. And as long as you don't hit the head or horns, what's the difference?"

"Yes," Slocum said. "As long as I knock it on its ass."

He took the cartridge and the Springfield and walked out of the fort. He took the road that led to Brown's Canyon. He stayed in the middle of the road. Just before it entered the canyon, he set a small white stone. No one was in sight. He turned and climbed the long slope, up through the chaparral, up to the pines growing along the ridge. He lay between two pines. Behind him, down the hill, there was plenty of room between the trees for a man to make good time on an Arabian mare. Then there came a flat of chaparral and an opening into a distant valley. It was ideal terrain for a fast getaway ride, Slocum thought with satisfaction.

Once more he scanned the terrain. Nothing was in sight. High above the ridge, two hawks circled in an updraft. The sky was an intense turquoise blue. Massive cumulus clouds drifted slowly by.

Slocum thought that it was a good day to practice killing a man. He rested the long barrel between his left thumb and forefinger. His hand would help absorb the shock of the explosion. He lined up the front bead with the rock. The rock was at a distance where elevated sights, if he were using a regular cartridge, would be necessary. Gravity would pull the bullet down long before it reached the target. If he used an elevated rear sight, the muzzle would not really be aimed at the target; it would be aimed upward. The bullet, in its flight from muzzle to target, would describe a parabola. And at this distance it would either fall short or, more likely, miss. Or a sudden wind gust might push it as much as seven or eight inches to one side.

But a powerful shove from an extrastrong explosive would eliminate the parabola. It would also cancel out the effect of a wind gust.

He tossed a grass blade in the air. It fell straight down. Good. With anticipation Slocum sighted the rock. He squeezed the trigger.

The latch blew off and gouged a three-inch track a quarter of an inch deep across his right cheekbone. The latch penetrated the trunk of a nearby pine tree. Slocum said, "Shit!" Of course, the Springfield had not been built to allow for such extreme pressure. It was stupid of him not to have figured that. He pressed his shirt against the gash till the blood clotted, and then he dug the latch out of the tree with his knife. It had gone in three inches. In a sense, the Springfield had fired two bullets, Slocum thought, with a grin. He walked down to the road. He could not find any trace of the bullet. He kicked the stone out of the road and walked back to the fort.

All the latch needed was another screw. He took it from Johansen's supply of nails and screws and gun parts. He put another cartridge inside and dropped the latch. This time he wound several turns of heavy wire around the latch and the breech.

He decided not to go back to Brown's Canyon. Someone might notice his two trips there and wonder what was going on. This time he took along a piece of burnt wood from the fireplace. Arriving at the firing range, he used the wood to trace the outline of a man's head and torso on the bull's-eye. Then he turned and walked back up the slope till he was in the same relative position he had been in at Brown's Canyon. He took off his shirt, folded it, and used it for a rest and a shock absorber. He aimed carefully at the center of the torso and squeezed the trigger. The bull's-eye exploded.

## 21

Nachodise, lying on his belly just below the ridge line, saw the bullet hit the bull's-eye. He had watched with grave interest as the tall white man with the beard and the bear-claw necklace prepared to fire.

Nachodise had found a retreat four miles away in a box canyon. He was roasting mescal in a pit, and he knew that he would eat well later on. He had no anxiety about where or what he would eat that night. He could give his undivided attention to the tall man and his doings. No smoke came from the rifle. That he had never seen! This man had very good medicine. He had already killed a bear with only a knife, and now he had a magic gun that fired bullets without smoke.

The bullets did much damage, more than Nachodise had ever seen. This was clearly a man whom it would be very hard to kill. A man could easily get killed himself if he were to try it.

Nachodise had been toying with the idea of killing Slocum when he retraced his steps back from the range. But now he decided that it would be too hard and too dangerous. It would be very sensible to let him alone. But, on the other hand, to kill a brave man with such strong medicine, *that* would be a feat to boast about during his old age. Nachodise sighed. Maybe he would try it another time. In his medicine bag back at the hidden box canyon he had a piece of wood from a tree that had been struck by lightning. He also had a small, heavy stone to which bits of iron would cling. Perhaps if he were to carry those and then run across the tall white man with the bear-claw necklace, he might have some good medicine himself.

Or he might get that woman with the long red hair. Nachodise had seen her once on the porch of her house before he had lost his binoculars. She had washed her hair and had stepped out and sat on the steps to dry it in the sun. Nachodise had never seen hair that color. It was the same shade as the poppies that filled the valleys in early April after a good, long winter rain. Apaches hardly ever took scalps, but he didn't mind making an exception for this one. It would look especially fine hanging from the head of his lance as he charged some wagonmaster. It would make even the Comanches jealous.

Nachodise was getting hungry. He slid down the ridge, discarded the camouflage screen of *sacaton* grass, and trotted back to his canyon. As he drew near, he could smell the roasting mescal roots. He began to salivate. Mescal and venison made a fine combination, and he hadn't eaten since the night before.

\* \* \*

Slocum stood up. He was satisfied that the Springfield worked perfectly. Relief flooded through him. He was tired of this place, tired of controlling his feelings whenever he saw Murray, tired of having to restrain himself at Morrissey's mockery. He would be pleased to get the whole thing over with and be on his way somewhere where he could make some real money.

He slung the rifle over his back and began walking back. He stopped suddenly, lifted his head, and took a deep breath. There was a faint whiff of roasting mescal. That meant only one thing: Apaches.

Apaches near the fort! Slocum thought that they were, very likely, a band with women. It was the women's job to cut up the tasty, nutritious plant. Slocum paused and thought hard. If they were close to the fort and cooking, it meant that they had no idea what Murray would do if he came across them. They were very likely an isolated little band that had no contact with any other group that might know about Murray's new and savage policy. Perhaps they were Mescaleros who had drifted down the mountain ranges of the continental divide.

Slocum sighed. He would have to warn them to get the hell away from the fort. He followed the aroma of the mescal, which was very faint. The air currents turned and twisted along the arroyos and canyons. From time to time he stopped and took another deep breath. The smell was getting stronger. Lizards scuttled out of his path. When he crossed a dry, sandy wash, a sidewinder whipped its wide S loops as it moved in its sinuous deadly way. A coyote panted in the shadow of a rock, watching Slocum's progress.

Slocum stopped. Ahead of him was a small box canyon. The smell was coming out of it, a mile or maybe a mile and a half inside. If he were to go in, and if they had a sentinel on duty who knew his business, he could die with an arrow transfixing his throat. It would then be too late to announce that his intentions were friendly.

Slocum withdrew carefully and then circled around till he saw an arroyo that seemed to run parallel to the box canyon. He followed it until he judged that he was opposite the mouth of the canyon. He looked up. The top seemed to be about a hundred feet high. The arroyo wall had been worn smooth by the passage of flood water over several thousand years. But when he came closer, he saw that it was not really vertical. There were little ledges, outcrops, and fissures. It seemed quite possible that he could climb up without too much difficulty. He flexed his hands, hoping that they had healed enough to take the strain he would subject them to.

Slocum pulled off his boots to get a better purchase with his bare feet. He tied the boots together and hung them from his belt. There was no way he could take the rifle. Its weight and the likely overbalancing it would cause might be fatal. He sighed and left it before starting to climb. It was easier than he had thought it would be. Little fingerholds and handholds were everywhere. Halfway up there was a ledge about three feet wide. He could rest there a while. He placed an arm full length on the ledge and prepared to hoist himself. He froze.

Slocum had heard the very distinctive sound of

dried peas being shaken. The sound came from the ledge. He couldn't whip his hand backward. That was his only grip; he would lose his balance and fall fifty feet. He had to keep the arm there. He closed his eyes and waited for the strike, but nothing happened. He pulled himself up to the ledge. Nothing was there. But at the rear of the ledge was a narrow, deep fissure. The rattler had retreated. Slocum let out a deep breath. He stood on the ledge and reached upward for another grip. He remembered suddenly that his feet were bare. He thought of Kazshe and the way she used to talk to rattlesnakes.

"Oh, I am sorry I disturbed you, my brother!" Slocum said in Apache. "I mean you no harm. Forgive me."

The snake did not strike.

Slocum reached the top of the cliff without any more problems. The land flattened out into a narrow mesa liberally strewn with cholla and pincushion cactus. He pulled on the boots and carefully approached the rim of the box canyon. Twenty feet away he took off his hat, and then he wriggled on his belly, aiming for a sagebrush that grew right on the rim edge. Once there, he peered through its densely matted branches, down into the box canyon.

Nachodise!

Slocum almost laughed aloud. Here was his enemy, completely defenseless. It would be easy to go back, climb down, get the Springfield, climb back up, and blow the man's chest wide open. Slocum could pay him back for the torture and the insults to which the big Chiricahua had subjected him. The round trip would take an hour. Nachodise liked to eat plenty. Slocum could see a venison haunch. There was a lot of mescal, and Nachodise always slept for a couple of hours after gorging himself, especially if he thought he was in a safe place.

But one thing held Slocum back. He would have to pass that rattlesnake ledge three more times in his comings and goings. The rattler—assuming that there was only one there—would not be satisfied with just a warning, particularly if Slocum's hand or foot came so close that the snake would assume that an attack was intended. And a rock like that, with a deep fissure, God! Slocum thought that there could be hundreds of diamondbacks coiling and slithering over one another inside the rock wall. And now that the air was cooling, they could be starting to emerge onto the ledge.

No, sir! Slocum thought. Too risky. This trip down would be the last one for the day. He made noises as he descended. He found a pebble and tapped it against the rock face so that the vibration would alert the diamondbacks that someone was coming. Slocum prayed that they would take the hint kindly and get out of the way.

When his bare feet neared the ledge where he had had the first encounter, he said, "Brother Rattlesnake, I mean you no harm."

He reached the bottom without incident. As he sat pulling on his boots, he began to laugh. He laughed so loud that he had to choke himself to silence lest the sound carry somehow to the neighboring box canyon and betray him the way that Nachodise's roasting mescal had given the Apache away.

"Nachodise," he said finally, standing up and slinging the rifle over his shoulder, "Brother Rattlesnake saved your life! Count yourself lucky today."

## 22

"How'd it work out?" Johansen asked.

"Fine, just fine," Slocum replied. He put the Springfield down. "A little trouble with the latch."

"So I see. I never thought about that happening. I'll make a note of that. If someone went and test fired it with that extraheavy charge, my name would be mud around Washington. Let me put some iodine on it."

"No, thanks," Slocum said. He hated the sting of iodine. "It's healin' all right."

"Well, all right." Johansen smiled in satisfaction. "Now, am I the world's greatest chemist or am I not?" he demanded. "We can safely say that I am!"

They were in the laboratory. "Before I leave—" Johansen went on, but Slocum interrupted.

"When'll that be?"

"Tomorrow morning bright and early. I'll get up with the little birds and give God the glory! Quick notice, eh? Murray's taking a patrol, so I'll have an escort as far as the railroad. Then it's ho! for Washington and a big contract!"

To get to the Southern Pacific tracks, the patrol would have to go through Brown's Canyon. Slocum had to act fast. He needed a good horse and one more specially built cartridge. That, he hoped, would be all that was necessary to take care of the major. The Springfield would be too bulky to handle from horseback in his escape, but it would have to do. Regular cartridges would be sufficient until he could pick up a Winchester. One thing he did not intend to do any more was unwind and wind the wire around the latch before and after each shot. That could become ridiculous if he were jumped by a war party of any size.

"Tell you what I'll do, Brian. I'll make up a batch of those high-velocity smokeless cartridges for you. You can go get yourself some target practice while I'm gone."

"I'll be grateful." That was a worry removed.

"Shucks. Now I'm getting to talk the way they do around here. Here's someone walking in the store. I can hear them overhead."

"I'll take care of them."

"Good, good. I'll get to work on your special order here."

Slocum, as always, moved silently. When he crossed the porch and entered the store, the ex-corporal Morrissey and his sidekick, a quiet German immigrant named Schildhaus, stood at the counter. Morrissey was placing two cans of peaches in his haversack. Schildhaus was munching on a cracker he had just taken from the cracker barrel.

Schildhaus was saying, "And tonight you curry der major's mare."

"Not me, Dutchy." Morrissey buckled the flap.

"Major said you do it."

"Curse the bitch! She bites me hands, she steps on me feet! Get someone else. Get that Riley lad. He grew up on a farm in County Mayo. The boy *likes* horses."

"The major says you."

"Schildhaus—"

"*Sergeant* Schildhaus. When you get your stripes back, all right, Schildhaus. And you don't want to do his horse, all you got to do is tell him. He's eatin'. Just go and knock at his door and say, 'Major, I don't want to curry your *verdammte* horse. You wipe your own *gottverdammte* horse!' Ja, I like to hear that." Schildhaus placidly munched at his cracker.

Morrissey cursed in a resigned manner.

Slocum stepped inside. He walked behind the counter and leaned on it.

"Well, look here!" Morrissey jeered. "What we got here? A real storekeeper!"

Slocum smiled. The thought of having Morrissey groom the major's mare, which he would then steal, struck him as a marvelous irony. His smile broadened as he thought of what Morrissey would say when he found out.

"What's funny, you hairy son of a bitch?"

Schildhaus stiffened. His jaws froze. Slocum's smile slowly faded. Morrissey dropped the haversack on the counter with a thump. He went into a prizefighter's crouch.

"Come on, come on!" he shouted, dancing lightly on the balls of his feet.

Oh, no, not now, not now when I'm so close to ending it, Slocum thought. The fool might ruin all his careful planning. Slocum feared his own violent temper. He had controlled it rather well, he thought, up to now, but this irritating bastard was getting to be too much of a burden for him to suffer in patience.

Schildhaus was a much better reader of faces than Morrissey. He called out warningly, "Morrissey! Don't be a stupid!"

"Got no stripes to lose, Schildhaus!" Morrissey said, exultant.

What about your life, *dumkopf*? Schildhaus wanted to say, but he remained quiet while Slocum stepped from behind the counter and took a step toward Morrissey. Schildhaus had seen the killer in Slocum's eyes, and now he knew that he had to act quickly. The German put a hand on Morrissey's sleeve in a warning move, but Morrissey shook it off.

"Come on, come on!" Morrissey chanted. "First, me boy, I'll break your nose. To start! Then I'll—"

"You'll start nothing here!" said Johansen. "You're a troublemaker. You start something, and I'll make damn sure you wind up in the guardhouse!"

"And that's what I'd like! No more goddamn patrols! So put them up!"

Johansen stepped in front of Slocum, blocking his slow, deadly approach toward Morrissey. "For a favor to me, Brian! I can't risk anything happening to you, not now, not when I'm leaving the place in your care."

Slocum stopped. He stared at Johansen for a moment. Then he shrugged. "Yes," he said. Then he added, "Mr. Morrissey here would like to pay you for the two cans of peaches in his haversack."

Morrissey glowered. Johansen as a witness would be too much to handle. He reluctantly set the money on the counter. Schildhaus grabbed him by the elbow and propelled him out the door.

"Thanks," Johansen said. He clapped Slocum on the back.

Slocum was trying to suppress his rage. It finally subsided. This was the first time in his life he had permitted that deadly insult to go unpunished. He did not like the flavor it left in his mouth. It made him almost nauseous. But the thought that he would eventually catch up with Morrissey made him feel somewhat better.

At supper he pretended to listen to Johansen's last-minute instructions. He nodded from time to time. He felt bad, knowing that he would have to betray the man's trust in him. It would be painful, but Slocum had made his choice. To kill Murray was more important. It was regrettable that Slocum would have to flee, since there was not much doubt that most of Johansen's stock would be looted before the officers realized that Bearclaw had taken off with the major's horse and left the store open to everyone.

Johansen got up and washed the dishes. He dried them on the old flour sack. Slocum suddenly realized that he would miss this simple routine and the relaxed talks he had had with Johansen.

"Last time I do these goddamn dishes," he said. "You're on your own till I come back."

He poured coffee into the two chipped china mugs, and the two men sat on the porch and watched the sun sink behind the ranges in a vast sea of orange fire.

"Such a pretty country!" Johansen said musingly. "You ought to see it round here in the spring. Indian paintbrush, balsam root, poppies, phlox—all blooming at once to get into seed before the heat comes. There's not a sight like it anywhere else! Well, it's time for an old man to get to bed. I'll leave before you get up. So I'll say good-bye now."

They shook hands warmly. Johansen set up his cot below the front window, which was his favorite place to catch any vagrant gust of air on hot nights. Slocum waited till Johansen's gentle snores began. Then he quietly got up and pulled out a pair of saddlebags he had bought cheaply from Johansen the week before in preparation for this night.

Opening the flaps, he inserted his bear-claw necklace, the money he had saved from the sale of the furs and his salary from Johansen, a few slices of beef, half a loaf of bread, some coffee, a brick of sugar, a frying pan, and a spoon and fork. He added a canteen, spare underclothes, a shirt, and a handful of cartridges.

Slocum picked up the Springfield. He had made a leather sling for it; now he attached it. He put on his hat and coat. He tiptoed past the deeply snoring Johansen, across the porch, and down the steps. A few lights shone in the officers' houses. All else was dark, except for the stable. There a disgruntled Morrissey was reluctantly grooming the major's fine Arabian mare, which Murray planned to ride on the morning's patrol.

Slocum decided that he would make Morrissey more disgruntled than ever. He put down his gear behind the stable where no one would see it. With the grace and silence of a mountain lion, he approached Morrissey.

The man was currying the mare viciously. Her coat was shiny and black as ebony. She was a beautiful horse, what the Navajos would call *nizhoni*. As Slocum neared Morrissey, the mare's ears flicked in his direction. Morrissey was a bad man for the frontier; he didn't notice the mare's movement.

"Dirty bitch, hold still, now!" he muttered.

Slocum's fist hit him in the back of the neck. As he pitched forward, Slocum pulled him around savagely and slammed him in the solar plexus. Morrissey was paralyzed. He went down on his knees. Slocum was tempted to identify himself for Morrissey's benefit but decided upon caution instead. He hit the man once more, this time on the point of the jaw. There was a solid click as his jaw snapped shut, and he toppled over unconscious. Now they were even.

Slocum shoved a dirty rag into his mouth. He tied it in place with another one. He tied Morrissey's hands and feet, dragged him to the far end of the stable, and pitched him into an empty stall. Someone would find him late in the morning.

Then he threw a saddle blanket over Fatima, Murray's mare, who seemed excited by the strange happenings. When Slocum petted her, she responded with an affectionate nudge. Slocum led her quietly out of the stable after he saddled her, threw the saddlebags on, and mounted. She quivered when he got on, but he soothed her and took her out of the fort at a walk. No one saw them. In an hour, he was on top of the ridge. Fatima was tethered fifty feet below, on the far side from the road that approached Brown's Canyon. She was happily munching oats in the nosebag he had stolen on the way out of the stable.

Slocum lay warm in his coat, waiting for sunrise and the patrol. He had rolled up his spare shirt for a gun rest. It would absorb the tremendous shock nicely. The Springfield, loaded with the huge cartridge, with the latch carefully wired, was trained on the road, just about where Murray would come to a halt while the scouts penetrated the canyon.

Slocum felt a very pleasant sense of anticipation in the predawn darkness. Three months was a long time to wait. He had accepted that delay in order to avenge the deaths of Kazshe and Dilchay. When this was over, perhaps within the hour—he already could see the rim of the sun sliding upward on the eastern horizon—he would be gone on the serious business of making a lot of money somewhere. But now he needed patience, until the time came to squeeze the trigger and send Major Murray to hell.

## 23

The morning dawned clear and without any wind. He would have no problem allowing for any sideward drift of the bullet. He waited patiently. Slocum knew how to wait. Below him, Fatima stamped and blew through her nose in a sign of contentment. All Slocum would have to do was shoot, grab his shirt, roll down the slope, mount, and take off.

By the time they figured out where the shot might have come from—and it would take plenty of time without the telltale smoke—he'd have a lead that their fourth-rate cavalry plugs would never be able to match. He'd sell Fatima in another territory, or even better, in Mexico. No one in Mexico would ask questions or even care who had owned Fatima earlier. The money he'd get for her would let him make a fresh start.

The patrol was coming into the valley at a fast trot. Slocum rubbed his hands to warm the fingers and make them limber. Murray believed in shaking everyone up in the morning. Or maybe he contemplated a long ride and wanted to cover plenty of ground by noon. When the major was a hundred yards from the opening of the canyon, Slocum cocked the Springfield and began leading slightly with the flat-topped front sight.

Murray slowed. He wanted to allow the Pima scouts to search the canyon and the cliffs on either side. Sibley, riding in front, raised his gloved hand. The column stopped. Sibley moved forward a bit, and the column automatically followed. Then Sibley turned and frowned and held up his hand again. The column halted. Sibley shook his head and waited for the scouts.

Slocum watched the Pima scouts as they rode along on the top of the white clay surface, one man on each side. They saw nothing there but the usual clumps of mesquite. Murray was blocked from Slocum's sight by the bodyguard surrounding him. Slocum prayed that they would shift position a bit when the scouts gave the go-ahead sign, letting him get in one good shot. Their horses were restless and kept shifting position. Murray's horse was restless as well. He probably was not used to being ridden by the major.

"God damn," Slocum whispered. He would have to make a snap shot at the very first opportunity. Sibley pumped his closed fist up and down. The column began to move forward. Slocum tightened his grip on the trigger, but before his forefinger had traveled an eighth of an inch, a part of the clay ledge seemed to disintegrate and launch itself at Murray. Slocum saw the movement out of the corner of his eye and froze. It was Nachodise. The

Apache had been waiting there since the night before; he was smeared with clay.

He plunged downward like a diver, his lance extended. The point entered Murray's throat just above the breastbone. Driven by Nachodise's heavy weight, the lance continued downward. It went through Murray, snapping his spine in two just above the cantle of the saddle. It angled downward still, through the cantle, and penetrated into the horse for five inches.

Murray was pinned to the saddle like a grotesque butterfly. He screamed. The horse, maddened by the pain, bucked violently across the road and slammed against the canyon wall.

Nachodise had fallen on his knees in the road after letting go of the lance shaft. He managed to get off one shot from Slocum's old Colt before he was riddled with bullets from the bodyguard's carbines. He lived only thirty seconds more than Murray, but he sang his death song triumphantly.

The patrol clustered around Murray. They dismounted and took defensive positions. They were sure an attack would follow, launched by a great war party of Chiricahua.

It was a good time to leave. Slocum hid everything under the branches of a fallen pine. There was no point going on as he had planned. He would ride back to the fort and say that he had found Fatima wandering past the firing range. He would say that he had found her riderless. After all, Morrissey had never seen the man who had knocked him unconscious. They would believe him. There was no reason to make up such a story.

He would be able to keep his promise to Johansen, thank God! He would run the store until the chemist came back from Washington. The lonely widow would require solace, and she would get all she could handle. Slocum knew that he would figure out a way to take care of Bailey. What the hell, Kazshe and Dilchay had been only half avenged. To kill the richest man in Arizona Territory—now, *that* would be something to work on.

# WE HOPE YOU ENJOYED THIS BOOK

IF YOU'D LIKE A FREE LIST
OF OTHER BOOKS AVAILABLE FROM
**PLAYBOY PAPERBACKS,**
JUST SEND YOUR REQUEST TO:
**PLAYBOY PAPERBACKS**
BOOK MAILING SERVICE
P.O. BOX 690
ROCKVILLE CENTRE, NEW YORK 11571

**GREAT WESTERN YARNS FROM ONE OF THE BEST-SELLING WRITERS IN THE FIELD TODAY**

# JAKE LOGAN

| | | |
|---|---|---|
| \_\_\_\_ | 16702 ACROSS THE RIO GRANDE | $1.50 |
| \_\_\_\_ | 16990 BLAZING GUNS | $1.95 |
| \_\_\_\_ | 21003 BLOODY TRAIL TO TEXAS | $1.95 |
| \_\_\_\_ | 21022 DEAD MAN'S HAND | $1.95 |
| \_\_\_\_ | 21006 FIGHTING VENGEANCE | $1.95 |
| \_\_\_\_ | 16939 HANGING JUSTICE | $1.95 |
| \_\_\_\_ | 16795 HELLFIRE | $1.95 |
| \_\_\_\_ | 16741 MONTANA SHOWDOWN | $1.75 |
| \_\_\_\_ | 21051 NORTH TO DAKOTA | $1.95 |
| \_\_\_\_ | 16979 OUTLAW BLOOD | $1.95 |
| \_\_\_\_ | 21159 RIDE FOR REVENGE | $1.95 |
| \_\_\_\_ | 16914 RIDE, SLOCUM, RIDE | $1.95 |
| \_\_\_\_ | 16935 ROUGHRIDER | $1.95 |
| \_\_\_\_ | 21160 SEE TEXAS AND DIE | $1.95 |
| \_\_\_\_ | 16866 SHOTGUNS FROM HELL | $1.95 |
| \_\_\_\_ | 21120 SLOCUM AND THE WIDOW KATE | $1.95 |

282-1

# JAKE LOGAN

| | | |
|---|---|---|
| ___ | 16880 SLOCUM'S BLOOD | $1.95 |
| ___ | 16823 SLOCUM'S CODE | $1.95 |
| ___ | 16867 SLOCUM'S FIRE | $1.95 |
| ___ | 16856 SLOCUM'S FLAG | $1.95 |
| ___ | 21090 SLOCUM'S GOLD | $1.95 |
| ___ | 16841 SLOCUM'S GRAVE | $1.95 |
| ___ | 21023 SLOCUM'S HELL | $1.95 |
| ___ | 16764 SLOCUM'S RAGE | $1.95 |
| ___ | 16863 SLOCUM'S RAID | $1.95 |
| ___ | 21087 SLOCUM'S REVENGE | $1.95 |
| ___ | 16927 SLOCUM'S RUN | $1.95 |
| ___ | 16936 SLOCUM'S SLAUGHTER | $1.95 |
| ___ | 21163 SLOCUM'S WOMAN | $1.95 |
| ___ | 16864 WHITE HELL | $1.95 |

1281-6

**PLAYBOY PAPERBACKS**
**Book Mailing Service**
P.O. Box 690  Rockville Centre, New York 11571

NAME_____

ADDRESS_____

CITY_____ STATE_____ ZIP_____

Please enclose 50¢ for postage and handling if one book is ordered; 25¢ for each additional book. $1.50 maximum postage and handling charge. No cash, CODs or stamps. Send check or money order.

Total amount enclosed: $_____